The Journey Goes On

The Journey Goes On

DAVID NIMMER

NODIN PRESS

Copyright © 1992 by David Nimmer

All rights reserved. No part of this book may be
reproduced in any form without the permission of
Nodin Press except for review purposes.

ISBN 0-931714-49-4

Nodin Press, a division of Micawber's Inc.
525 North Third Street
Minneapolis, MN 55401

Contents

PREFACE: MY MOMENTS   5

PART I: THE SECRET BOAT
    The Secret Boat   9
    Two Boys in the Big City   13
    Chipmunk   17
    Aunt Orma   21

PART II: AND WHO MIGHT YOU BE?
    And Who Might You Be?   27
    A Tough Cop   29
    Me and the Bear   33
    White House Briefing   35
    Live Shot, Slow Death   39
    A Wounded Eagle   43
    Musk Ox   45
    The Hunt for *Yankee Girl*   49
    A Pair of Haircuts   53
    A Damn Good Painter   57

PART III: THE RIGHT WOMAN
    The Right Woman   63
    My French Masterpiece   65
    In the Mountains   69
    Waiting for the Train   75
    Becker the Cat   79
    North Shore Rituals   83

PART IV: THE FORMULA
    The Formula   89
    The Shore-Lunch Gang   93
    A Sparrow among Cardinals   97
    Big Brother   99
    A Pocket Knife   101
    The Last Fishing Trip   103
    Handful of Memories   107

My Moments

Soon after I left WCCO Television news and was edging up on my fiftieth birthday, I started thinking about, brooding about, what I'd done with my life. I'd spent twenty-six years in journalism at the Minneapolis Star and the WCCO television newsroom, and I was used to the bylines and reporter stand-ups and all of the hoopla, hype, and notoriety that went along with them. Then one day I was in a line at a suburban supermarket when the checkout clerk gave me a quizzical look and said, "Say, didn't you used to be somebody on TV?" I nodded and told her that now I was about to start teaching journalism at the University of St. Thomas. On the way home I began logging a few of "my moments."

At first I had a one about army basic training and another about my first newspaper assignment. I wrote the titles down in a notebook, and by the end of the year I had a dozen story ideas. Then my wife Kris and I were invited to a New Year's Eve party where everyone was to tell a story. I wrote about an out-of-work house painter I had met at a food shelf and shelter. In the following months I wrote more, when we went on trips, when we relaxed at our North Shore hideaway, when I had an hour or two between classes. All these stories are true, though embellished here or there as part of the storyteller's art.

Part I

The Secret Boat

The Secret Boat

It was one-hundred-percent predictable that Bob and I would want a boat. We were classmates and best buddies who shared a love for everything from Boy Scouts to baseball. But what we loved most of all was the water. We'd stand on the banks of the Fond du Lac River to catch bullheads. We'd sit for hours at Lakeside Park, with cane poles and a bucket of minnows, to catch a northern pike.

Our hometown was at the bottom of Lake Winnebago, which stretches forty miles from north to south, five miles from east to west. That was big enough to set a couple of kids to dreaming about what they could see if they ever had a boat seaworthy enough to take a trip around that lake. Our problem, of course, was that our folks didn't want us to have a boat. We asked, once, twice, a half-dozen times. The answer was always no.

At the beginning of the summer between our sophomore and junior years, we spotted the boat for us. Riding our bikes past an old boat house, we saw this boat on a pair of sawhorses with a hand-lettered For Sale sign. She wasn't too impressive: a wooden-strip boat, a shade over fourteen feet long, with a rather narrow beam. The paint was peeling off, the caulking in the seams was flaking away, and a few boards in the transom were showing signs of dry rot.

Nonetheless, we found the owner and inquired as to the price. "She'll cost you thirty-five dollars, boys," he said. But he didn't say we needed our parents' permission. We'd told him we'd get back to him.

"Jeez, Nim," Bob said, "maybe this is our only chance to get a boat." The money wasn't a problem, since both of us worked at the newspaper, Bob delivering papers and I as an office boy.

The Journey Goes On

We were back at the marina the next day, with thirty-five dollars in cash. We plunked our money down on the counter and told the owner we wanted the boat.

"Okay, boys," he said. And then he paused, as though he might ask whether our folks knew about this.

"The boat'll be a gift to our fathers," Bob said. "We're going to fix it up and give it to them at Christmas." The owner took our money and gave us a receipt.

"Since this is a surprise," I said, "we'd like to leave the boat out here to work on it. Would that be all right?" He said it would.

We owned a boat. And we didn't feel a bit guilty about conning the marina owner: he must have known the truth.

We were out there every day. We scraped and sanded the hull. We caulked the seams. We brushed and washed the inside. And then we painted it red above the splash rail, gray below. The first coat soaked right into the dry wood and left a streaked finish. We sanded that down and applied a second coat. Now she was beginning to look like something.

We waited a couple of days for the second coat to dry and decided we were ready to launch. To christen her, we swung a bottle of Pepsi at the boat a half-dozen times and only chipped the paint. We settled on pouring the Pepsi over the bow. The marina man had given us a tiny slip at one end of the channel, and he helped us drag the boat into the water. She started to leak immediately. Fortunately, we knew that it took a day or two for a boat to soak up, for the wood to swell and tighten the seams. Once our craft had tightened up, she never leaked a drop. Now we bought a twenty-two-year-old Evinrude, with the flywheel on top and a separate starter cord. That old motor would wheeze and sputter, but it was a runner.

We went out in our boat two or three times a week. We went fishing, we went exploring, we just went riding. It was great. We owned something, something we'd fixed up, something that was secret. We bought running lights because part of our dream was to take her around the lake, and for that we'd have to run at night. We got a map of the lake and figured out how far we could go in a day and where we could stop at night. I've never found anything more exciting than our weeks of planning that trip.

We never did take it, though, because of work and family vacations. But our daily excursions provided all the excitement we could handle. There was the day we caught walleyes and white bass out on the reef. And there was the windy morning when the motor stopped and we blew into a concrete retaining wall on shore, without serious damage to the hull.

When school started in the fall, we didn't use the boat much. One Friday night we took it up the river, almost to the football field where our team played. But then we didn't use it again until late October, during the teachers' convention, when we took the boat across the lake to a cabin where we had permission to campout overnight. We got up early that morning and went out on the mist-shrouded lake. She could still take the wind and the waves and never leak a drop.

Before we went back home, however, we pulled the boat up in the brush along a sandy shoreline into a temporary hiding place about a quarter of a mile from where we'd camped. We still didn't know what we were going to do with the boat for the winter.

About a week later at suppertime Bob phoned. "Take a look at the want ads in the paper," he said. "Seek owner. A fourteen-foot wooden boat, red and gray, has been found on the West Shore, south of Black Wolf Point. The boat was pulled into the brush, apparently abandoned. Party with proof of ownership should call Fond du Lac County Sheriff's Office."

It was our boat, all right. But there was no way we could claim it. We didn't have the receipt anymore, and, besides, the sheriff would notify our folks.

Dad was reading the paper that night at supper. "Somebody left a boat in the brush on the West Shore. Why would any damn fool do something like that?"

I never gave him an answer. But I had one: Don't worry, they got their money's worth, every penny.

11

Two Boys in the Big City

We'd get down to the train station early in the morning on the day we were leaving for Chicago. It was a big deal for Bob and me to spend several days of our spring vacation out of town. We had been only fourteen years old when we started these spring trips, and our folks weren't exactly the kind to neglect looking after us. Bob and I were each the only children in our respective families, and as a result our leashes were never long enough to suit us. Somehow, for some reason, two pairs of conservative church-going parents from Fond du Lac, Wisconsin, had agreed that their sons could travel the one hundred twenty miles south to the city they had read about in Carl Sandburg's poem.

Waiting on that platform for the Chicago and Northwestern Four Hundred, the fastest and fanciest passenger train in the whole world, always made us antsy, looking up the tracks for that headlight. When we'd see it and then hear the rumble of the train, the adventure was about to begin. We'd step up into the coach and make our way to a pair of seats, just as though we were businessmen off on a sales trip. Bob and I always dressed up to travel in our only suits, with neckties and well-shined shoes. We didn't want to be mistaken for small-town kids who didn't know anything about worldly ways.

We did have a few things to learn about eating in the dining car. We liked having lunch while watching the meadows, fields and hardwoods of the Wisconsin countryside whiz by. We liked the luxury of the linen tablecloth, real silverware, and fresh flowers in a vase. At first, when the waiter served the finger bowls, each with a slice of lemon floating on the water, we weren't sure what to do. Is it a broth? Do you drink it? Then we noticed a man at a nearby table dip his fingers into the bowl, swish them around, and wipe them with his napkin. We could handle that.

By the time we got off the train at the LaSalle Station, we were always feeling pretty confident. At the Sherman Hotel, if the room they gave us was too small or was next to the elevator shaft, we knew enough to ask for a different room. But the people at the Sherman were always good to us, and they treated us as adults—called us Sir, addressed us as Mr. And on those few occasions when someone didn't, we took care of it.

For instance, there was a certain waitress in one of the hotel's fancier restaurants. Now, Bob and I liked to go to good restaurants. We had become acquainted with lobster tail and steak when we were twelve, so for us dinner in Chicago wasn't hamburgers and french fries. This waitress patronized us, as though she thought we might have wandered into the wrong room. "You boys understand this is a dinner menu only?" Of course, we understood. Would we be wearing suits and ties if we thought this was a lunch counter? Her service was slow, sloppy, and sarcastic. When it came time to pay for our expensive dinner, we counted out the tab to the exact penny and left it on the table with no tip.

I had had to go to the men's room to get my share of the dinner bill. My dad believed it was easy to have your pocket picked in Chicago, so my mother sewed a pocket into my shorts to keep the ten and twenty dollar bills. Bob carried all his money in his wallet, and it was never stolen. He didn't have to undress to pay for dinner.

After dinner we always changed to our jeans to wander the downtown streets at night. This part we never talked about with our folks in our phone calls home every other day. We'd walk around Rush Street at night, looking at the people, the partiers, and the cops, in their powder-blue squad cars.

With all of its clubs and joints, Rush Street had great music. In the springtime they left the doors open, so we could stand outside and listen. On one block you could hear a jazz quartet, on another a Dixieland band, and on another a blues trio. It was on Rush Street that I first heard Satin Doll and Take Five. Sometimes it was two or three in the morning before we'd return to the hotel, tired but still excited.

We'd leave a wake-up call because there was plenty to see during the day, stuff we could tell our folks about, like the Museum of Science and Industry and the Shedd Aquarium and the Museum of Natural History. And what stuff: a human fetus in a bottle, a sand shark on a coral reef, and a brontosaurus in wood, wire, and papier-mâché. We walked the hallways of the giant exhibitions for hours. We never bought anything to take home.

When we boarded the train, we took back memories, occasions, experiences. One of them was the trip out of town as the Four Hundred whizzed past tenements on Chicago's northside: layer after layer of back porches with kids on the stairways and clothes on the railings. The kids were mostly black and looked poor.

Some of them waved as the train went by.

Chipmunk

I'd always assumed army boot camp would be like a Boy Scout excursion. We'd take hikes, walk through the woods, cook over an open fire, and sleep on the ground, although I was never deluded enough to think we'd sing songs around the camp fire.

I was distinctly distressed, depressed, and disappointed after my first four days of army basic training at Fort Leonard Wood, Missouri. My high-school buddy Bob and I had spent the whole time in the holding barracks, awaiting assignment to our basic-training company, picking up cigarette butts and weeding the scruffy rock gardens around post headquarters. I was scared most of the time. Then the bus took Bob and me to Charlie Company, where we were ordered to report to the dayroom and fall out to an assembly area when our names were called.

"Nimmer, David H.," bellowed the company first sergeant.

I stumbled off the dayroom steps with my duffel bag over my shoulder. The bag weighed about half as much as I did, so I found it difficult to stop. I tumbled to the ground, picked myself up, and realized that I didn't know where to go. The other recruits were standing in even ranks and I didn't know whether to fall in at the end of the first line or start a new one at the back of the troop. I hesitated a little too long.

"Trooper! You—running around like a chipmunk. Get your ass over here! Now!"

I looked up into the unsmiling face of my platoon sergeant—my mother, father, brother, and confessor for the next eight weeks. Sergeant Richard N. Hollis wasn't tall, but he was considerably taller than my five and a half feet, and he had big shoulders, thick forearms, a square jaw, and piercing eyes.

"Damn, troop, you're just a runt, aren't you? You know, I'm

tired of getting saddled with all the misfits in my platoon. And now I've got you, a damned chipmunk. Well, stay out of my way, boy, and pay attention."

The next day Sergeant Hollis took us out for a marching lesson. He had a bass drum in the rear and counted cadence. "Left, right, left! Go to your left, your right, your left."

I was getting into the swing of this when my bootlace came untied. I hopped along, trying to tie it.

Something crashed down on the top of my helmet liner. I looked around and there was Sergeant Hollis with his helmet in his hand. "Keep your eyes up, chipmunk!" he hollered. "I don't want my troops looking on the ground."

I figured an explanation was useless, so I marched and hopped for the next half mile. I did keep my eyes up, because his whack on my head had broken the straps on my helmet liner, which now rested on my shoulders, making me look like a turtle. The only way I could see was to keep my head up.

In the following weeks I managed to survive without further attention, though I blundered with the "buddy shots," our practice for administering shots of atropine in a nerve-gas attack. My buddy was Bob. We sat opposite each other on chairs in a gymnasium, with our pants dropped around our ankles. Our practice syringes were filled with sugar water. You had to poke your syringe in the other guy's thigh, squeeze out the contents, and withdraw the needle. Done quickly, it's relatively painless. On the count of three Bob jammed his syringe into my thigh. It felt like a mosquito bite. When my turn came, I stopped the needle about a quarter of an inch above Bob's thigh and then eased it slowly into his flesh. In the seven years I'd known him, I'd never seen such a look of pain, which quickly turned to anger. The bruise on his thigh lasted a month.

By the end of basic training, I'd marched ten miles carrying my pack and M-1 rifle. I'd crawled the infiltration course, neither scared by the machine-gun fire nor nicked by the barbed wire. And I'd qualified as an expert marksman—not bad for a kid who'd never gone deer hunting. But no one seemed to notice how hard I was trying.

The Journey Goes On

On the last weekend of basic training, on my way to the post exchange, I ran into Sergeant Hollis, in his civilian clothes.

"Chipmunk," he said.

Here we go, I thought—one last ass chewing before we get rid of each other.

"Nimmer, I know I've ragged on you. And you're still a runt, you know. But you're also a man, and you proved it."

Looking straight into his face, I detected a hint of a smile.

Aunt Orma

When I was a kid, you never knew when Aunt Orma would show up. She lived in Minneapolis, three hundred miles from our southeastern Wisconsin home, so her visits were two or three years apart. But no one in the family ever heard from her between visits, and no one ever knew when she was coming. One day there'd be a phone call from her, and what a scramble that would start.

My grandmother, who was a half sister to Orma, would call Mother. "She's here," Grandma would say, "and I wonder whether she's bringing anybody with her." Orma occasionally traveled in the company of a man. In the 1940s and early 1950s single women didn't generally travel across state lines with a man, at least not in our family.

One summer Orma showed up with a former semipro baseball player called Mac. When she introduced him to the family, Orma ignored the silent evaluations. "It's good to see all of you," she said. "We just had to stop."

I was always glad to see Orma, who had an infectious zest for life. Maybe that was what Mac and Orma had in common—Orma didn't care much for baseball. But I did, and that produced an instant friendship with Mac, who taught me the intricacies of a smooth level swing. He tied a ball to our clothesline with a piece of string and had me swing at that ball again and again.

"Smooth and easy, Davey boy. The idea is to relax, keep your eye on the ball, and swing easy. There's nothing to it, lad—just you and the ball." Mac had a way of helping me relax. He wasn't as intimidating as my dad or the grim-faced Little League coach. And he'd been there, playing baseball under the lights on a small-town field. Had Mac stayed around awhile, he might have cured my nervousness at the plate. But after a couple of days Orma announced it was time to go home. Orma never stayed very long. She soon had heard enough gossip and had caught up on enough family history.

Orma had a job to support herself. Her first husband had died when they were both in their early twenties. Orma had then taken a job as a tailor—not a seamstress, mind you, but a tailor. She didn't get much time off, so I took it as an honor when she phoned one summer and asked if I wanted to come to Minneapolis. I was twelve at the time, and I'd never traveled by myself. My folks were hesitant, but Orma persuaded them. She'd meet me at the train station, and I'd stay at her place. It would be good for me to develop a sense of independence. Orma knew how to deal with the family conservatism.

That trip was my first out-of-town adventure. Orma took me downtown to see the Foshay Tower, at thirty-one stories a skyscraper to me. The sports shop on the first floor had more rods and reels than I'd ever seen, and it had a freezer with the "biggest fish of the week." Orma took me to see the Mississippi River, to the movie *The Caine Mutiny*, and to meet the governor at the State Capitol, but Orville Freeman was out of town. Best of all, we stopped at a bar in Saint Paul for a hamburger with fried onions and a dill pickle, the biggest and best hamburger I ever had. I felt pretty grown up, eating in a working man's bar.

I didn't see Orma much in my high-school and college years, but I thought of her when I saw that the *Minneapolis Star* was one of the recruiters at the University of Wisconsin School of Journalism. Would Orma remember me? I phoned her. "Oh Lordy, of course I remember you. I meant to write, but I was never good at letters. So how are you and what's on your mind?" I told her that I might interview with the Minneapolis newspaper, and I asked whether she thought it was a good idea. "It'd be fine to have you in this town, and I think you'd like my husband." Orma had married again, almost forty years since her husband had died.

I got the job, and when I arrived in Minneapolis, I stayed with Orma and her husband Courtney until I found my first apartment. The two of them were like old cats sharing the same space, spitting and snarling at each other once in a while. Orma and Courtney bragged they never went to bed angry. They also never let a week go by without phoning to see how the rookie reporter was doing in the big city.

When Courtney died, Orma said she was through with marriage. She didn't want to go through the pain of losing another husband. She filled her life with reading and visiting and sewing and knitting and traveling. She went to Hawaii when she was almost ninety and she traveled in a camper to a family reunion in Oregon when she was ninety-three.

Orma continued to be a source of energy and courage for me. When I felt shame and failure over my divorce, she told me I'd been as good a married man as she'd ever met. When I trembled at the thought of leaving the newspaper and, ten years later, leaving the television station to teach, she told me to take the risk. "You follow this," she'd say, pointing to her stomach, the source of her gut hunches. "We really know what we want to do. We just got to have the gumption to do it." Whenever I left one of those sessions in her living room, I wondered why I'd been agonizing.

Orma lived in her high-rise apartment for twenty-five years, surviving cancer surgery, bruised ribs, and a broken hip. Because of the broken hip, she couldn't stay on her feet without assistance or a railing on the wall. She never seemed to hold it against me that I'd suggested it was time to move to a nursing home.

On a visit there, I remarked that the place seemed pleasant and everyone seemed friendly. I said I'd heard the food was getting better. She listened and when I was through, we sat in silence.

"This place is okay," she said finally, "but it's not like being home. You do everything when they tell you. You eat what they serve you. And the way they serve you—you know what that's like? Yesterday they served a dinner with beets, and they plopped the beets on my plate so the juice ran all over the mashed potatoes." She paused and then said, "But that's just the way of things. And what a body has to do is make the best of it."

Part II

And Who Might You Be?

And Who Might You Be?

Sitting at my desk at the end of the newsroom, struggling with an obituary, I was painfully aware that I hadn't set the world on fire in my first two weeks as a reporter at the *Minneapolis Star*. My one and only suit was fraying at the cuffs. One of the veteran reporters had mistaken me for a copy boy and sent me up to the city desk with a take of her story. The city editor had hollered across the room at her, "Damn it, he may not look like it, but he is—repeat—*is* a reporter." The whole experience had been reminiscent of army boot camp, with editors instead of sergeants. At least in basic training everyone else was a rookie too.

I was jolted out of my depression by a crisp shout from the city editor. "Nimmer, we got a dead body out near the Old Soldier's Home. Figures that it's an old soldier. So find out who he is and how he died."

This was my chance to show the desk that this rookie knew what to do. I grabbed the keys to the company cruise car, ran down three flights of stairs, and backed the battered compact out of its parking stall. In my haste to get away I tore the head bolt heater cord from the old car. And as I rolled out onto the street, I realized I didn't have the faintest idea where the Old Soldier's Home was. I raised a copy boy on the two-way radio for directions.

This Old Soldier's Home was next to a city park, and the body was at the bottom of a hill, at the end of a toboggan slide. From the hilltop I saw a cluster of top-coated detectives at the bottom. I was wearing a trench coat and a hat, to look taller and older, and I was carrying a ballpoint pen and several sheets of folded copy paper. On the second or third step on the icy toboggan slide, I fell, lost my hat, dropped my notepaper and ballpoint, and slid.

At the bottom I shot past the yellow tape marking the border of the crime scene. Coming to a stop in disarray, I looked up into the unsmiling round face of the city's ace homicide detective. He removed his cigar from his mouth, paused, and said, "And who might you be?"

I struggled to my feet and brushed the snow from my sleeve. "I'm from the *Minneapolis Star*."

"How long you been with them?"

"Two weeks."

"Would you like to live long enough to make it three?"

I nodded, and he invited me to step out of the crime scene. As I moved aside, I sputtered that this was my first real assignment.

"Okay," he said, "let me tell you what I know." I had to borrow some notepaper from him and then I scribbled furiously. The victim was a fourteen-year-old girl who'd been stabbed in the back some forty times and bashed in the head with a tire iron. According to some witnesses, the victim and her boyfriend had been arguing the night before and had gone for a walk in the park.

I scrambled up the hill and got on the car radio to the city desk. "I'm here," I babbled, "and I got the details. It's a murder."

The city editor interrupted: "Don't tell the whole world about it. Get to a telephone and call rewrite."

Two blocks away at a gas station, I used the pay phone and, shivering in the cold, reported my story to a rewrite man. "And so the police are speculating," I concluded, "that it's a crime of passion since she was stabbed so many times."

The city editor asked, "Did you get somebody to confirm the fact this is a homicide?"

"Well, no," I replied, wondering how it could be anything but.

I went back for an official confirmation. My new friend the homicide detective was still there.

"Excuse me," I said, "but can you tell me for the record that this is a homicide?"

He took the cigar from his mouth, and spat in the snow.

"No, kid," he drawled, "for the record this is the goddamnedest suicide I've ever seen."

Then, luckily for me and my future as a reporter, he smiled.

A Tough Cop

From the first week I met him in the Minneapolis police headquarters, he called me Short Shit. And in the succeeding years he found occasion to cut my brand-new tie in half, handcuff me to the top drawer of my pressroom desk, and introduce me to people as his illegitimate son. But I never had a better source, or one I cared more for, than Donald R. Dwyer.

When we met, I was a twenty-two-year-old police reporter, and he was a veteran detective, about to become a deputy chief, with a square jaw, a ruddy complexion, and an ever-present Palma Throw-Out cigar sticking from the corner of his mouth. He was blunt, forceful, aggressive, confident, and sometimes outrageous. He thrived in crises: sticky disciplinary cases, fights with the police union, and confrontations with angry mobs.

I remember Dwyer standing in the middle of Plymouth Avenue during the 1967 riots. He was the acting chief, in command of several hundred anxious and mostly young policemen on a hot and muggy Thursday night in July. Racial tensions and frustrations had exploded into violence. Stores were burning. Rocks had been thrown. Guns had been fired. Someone hurled a chunk of concrete that tore off the top of a phone booth in which I was reporting to my editors. I ran down the middle of the avenue, terrified, and almost crashed into Dwyer, standing in the street next to a squad car. He pulled the cigar from his mouth.

"Running a qualifying heat, Short Shit?"

I told him there was nothing funny about it. I blurted out the story of the concrete, the exploding phone booth and the flying glass.

"Settle down, Shorty. We will survive." He clapped his hands and said that this was one of life's moments. Where else would we choose to be than right in the middle of it?

In retrospect, that may sound grandiose, but at the time his words were strangely comforting. And so was his performance. He never turned his police force loose on the rioters, for which restraint he was criticized later. The damage was confined to Plymouth Avenue, the looting was minimal, and no one was killed.

At a lunch twenty-one years later, we talked about that night. Dwyer had insisted that Jack McCarthy and I meet him for lunch. Jack and Dwyer had been Minneapolis police colleagues, and they were friends who knew enough about each other's frailties to have few pretenses. We sat in one of those trendy, fern-filled, suburban eateries where the accessories are mix-and-match and the hamburgers cost seven bucks. The conversation had been inconsequential, the sentences trailing off and fading away. Finally Jack could stand it no longer.

"You look awful," he told Dwyer. "How bad is it?"

Dwyer smiled. "I'm still breathing," he said, "but that's about all." He'd had heart attacks and coronary-bypass surgery several years earlier. But now his heart muscle was so badly damaged that doctors felt a heart transplant was his only hope. "I'll be damned, Jack," he said, "but I'm not going to do that." He didn't want to take a handful of pills every day or visit the clinic once a week for blood tests or check in at the hospital every three months for a transplant-rejection examination. And he didn't relish long walks or leafy vegetables or high-fiber food or life without a good cigar.

Then Dwyer laughed with a cackle. "Say, Jack, do you remember the time ?" And the two of them told stories about cops they knew, cases they'd worked on, and street characters they'd met. The conversation was funny and alive and full of the judgments of two old police bulls who didn't give a damn what anybody thought. Dwyer picked up the check.

Jack and I gave him a ride the few blocks back to his condominium. McCarthy said goodbye and stayed in the car, and I walked with Dwyer to the lobby. He could barely climb the three-step stairway. We stood for a moment just inside the door. Background music was playing, and a young man, an assistant manager, was sitting behind a desk.

"Take care," I said, "I'll see you in a couple of weeks when I get back from vacation."

"Maybe, Shorty," he said, "and maybe not." He turned and walked away.

One week later as my wife and I headed west on Highway I-94 to begin our vacation, I flipped on the radio for the news: "Former Minneapolis Police Chief Donald Dwyer died today at Abbott Northwestern Hospital. Dwyer, known for his blunt and outspoken manner, had been in failing health for several months."

Suddenly, I wished I'd given him a hug.

Me and the Bear

It had been a tough spring for me and the Bear. My marriage of three years was falling apart right in front of the whole newsroom at the *Minneapolis Star*. Sue and I were both reporters there, and the feelings weren't easy to hide. I'd moved out of our luxury apartment into a one-room efficiency about a mile away. My new quarters were equipped with cockroaches, a balky toilet, a rock-hard couch that doubled as a bed, and one window, overlooking the Dempster Dumpster in the alley. I went to sleep to the clicking of cockroaches and woke up to a sunrise over the garbage bags. The vibrations in that pad were so deadly that my twenty-dollar Boston fern curled up and died in less than a week.

One of the few friends I had told about my new apartment and my separation from Sue was the Bear, so when his first wife decided she'd had enough and called off the marriage, the Bear knew where to come. He spent a couple of nights sleeping in a down bag on the floor . Even the Bear, with his tendency toward denial and his penchant for euphoria, had to admit it was a depressing forty-eight hours.

The Bear and I didn't do much more than struggle for the next several months. He found a little apartment in south Minneapolis. I bought a saucepan big enough to hold a cooking pouch. We told each other at least once a week that things were going to get better.

In early June Sue and I agreed that only a divorce made sense: we couldn't put the pieces back together. That decision left me relieved but very sad. I couldn't sleep that night, so I called the Bear just before midnight. "Let's get together tomorrow morning, early, and just bullshit." He said he had a busy day ahead but would stop by and pick me up at five in the morning.

The Journey Goes On

When my alarm went off at four-thirty, I decided for some reason to get all dressed up, not in my usual coat and tie and blue jeans but my newest and sportiest outfit: white shirt, pastel tie, dark blue slacks, blue and white seersucker sport coat, and bright white bucks. It was a beautiful morning of blue skies and a light breeze, so the Bear and I headed for Lake Harriet. We had the lake to ourselves and sat on a bench next to one of the walking paths.

I told the Bear that Sue and I had agreed to divorce, and I added that I was a little scared. For the next hour we watched the sun come up and tried to find some positive ways of dealing with the months ahead.

We were still chatting away when we noticed someone in a wheelchair rolling toward us down the path to our left. He was a young man in his late twenties. He was wearing a sleeveless undershirt and a forehead sweatband, but the sweat still dripped from his nose and chin. His shorts revealed the stocking-covered stumps of his legs. The poor bastard, I thought, he's a Vietnam casualty.

"Good morning, gentlemen," he said, slightly out of breath. "Isn't it a great day to be alive?" Without pausing for an answer, he rolled on down the path.

The Bear and I looked at each other. Someone had to say the obvious.

"And we think we've got troubles," I mumbled. The Bear nodded and smiled.

White House Briefing

I arrived in Washington in plenty of time to check into the Hay Adams Hotel, have an expensive dinner, and read the *Post*. At eight-thirty in the morning, I and twenty-three other editors and managing editors of newspapers around the country would be at the White House for a briefing from several of the President's cabinet officers and for a press conference with Jimmy Carter himself. The idea was that by hosting monthly media gatherings, the Carter administration could put its spin on its programs, such as energy conservation, and learn what folks were thinking in the hinterland. And the editors could play big shot and write about the briefing and the questions they asked the President. At the time I was the managing editor of the *Minneapolis Star*, and my goals were modest: I didn't want to embarrass myself by sounding ignorant and I wanted to shake the President's hand, and I wanted to take home some kind of souvenir from the White House.

The morning began in the Executive Office Building, adjacent to the White House. I was there at eight o'clock, a half hour before anyone would give us credentials. Looking around the assembled group and judging from the gray hair, I concluded that the majority of the editors must have been at least ten years older than I. Damn, I thought, maybe I should have worn the gray pinstripe instead of the brown sport coat. In the first briefing an assistant in the State Department described the prospect for improved relations with the Soviet Union. I was trying to remember which Roman numeral belonged with which SALT conference, so I could ask an intelligent question, when the session suddenly ended.

The second briefing was from an assistant secretary in the Department of Housing and Urban Development. She talked about housing blight, the problem with absentee landlords, and a new program using federal money to rehabilitate inferior housing stock. I knew something about cities and housing, having covered the Minneapolis City Council. Several of the editors asked about pretty obvious stuff. But this briefing ended while I was trying to remember whether it was called a "community development block grant" or a "community block grant development."

For our preluncheon press conference with President Carter, we trooped across the lawn to a side door of the White House and were ushered to the cabinet room with its large oblong table. The midday sunlight streaming in the windows gave the room a luminous glow. We sat around the table where the likes of Griffin Bell, Joe Califano, and Cyrus Vance gave their advice and consent. I was seated in one of the straight-back chairs along the walls. That increased my feeling of insecurity, and though I was thoroughly charmed by President Carter, I asked him not a single question, although as we left the room, I introduced myself, shook his hand, and told him I shared his love of fishing.

At our editors' lunch back in the Executive Office Building, I sat next to an editor from the *New York Post* or *Daily News*. He was wearing a black suit with a vest and a red carnation in his lapel. He had asked plenty of questions at the briefings.

I introduced myself and chattered for several minutes about my job with the *Star*. He never showed the slightest interest. To engage him in a journalistic issue, I asked him whether he thought the New York papers had been too lurid and sensationalistic in their coverage of the Son of Sam serial killer. A young man had recently been arrested, and some of the papers were publishing excerpts from his diary.

The editor looked up from his salad and stared at me. "No," he said, "I don't think the papers have been too lurid or sensationalistic. Maybe it's just that there's a lot of difference between life in New York City and life out there on the prairie."

I continued eating my lunch in silence. Then a man walked into the room and looked around. "Is Dave Nimmer here?" I raised my hand. He said to me, "The Vice President would like to see you." He was Al Eisele, Vice President Walter Mondale's

The Journey Goes On

press secretary. Obviously his office had a list of the editors at the briefing and had noticed the Minnesota connection. My luncheon companion looked at me in amazement. I said nothing and left the room with Eisele.

The Vice President, he explained, had a fifteen-minute break in his schedule and wanted to meet me. Fritz Mondale and I talked of Minnesota politics, his role in administration policy making, his support for the Wild Rivers' Act, and our shared concern for the outdoors. We walked for a few minutes in the Rose Garden and stepped into the President's empty office, where Mondale gave me a matchbook with the Presidential seal.

When I returned to the luncheon, the New York editor was still there. As I sat down, he leaned toward me. "What did he want?"

I looked at him for a moment. "I'm not sure I can explain it to you," I said. "You see, there's a lot of difference between life out there on the prairie and life in New York City."

Live Shot, Slow Death

I was a little cocky after a month as a rookie television reporter at WCCO. Actually, I wasn't exactly a rookie since I'd been in the news business for fifteen years at the *Minneapolis Star*. But what I knew about television in general and about being live on camera in particular left a lot to be desired, as I was soon to discover.

It had been a busy day at the station, with too many breaking news stories and too few reporters to cover them. "Nim," said Skip Loescher, "I'm out of bodies, and I need a live shot at six from the State Capitol. Could you do it?"

Well, how are you going to tell the assistant news director that you're a bit scared of live television? "Sure, Skip," I said, "just tell me what you want."

He explained that the issue was a House debate on the Mandatory Deposit Bill, which was intended to encourage the use of returnable glass bottles instead of disposable aluminum cans. The debate over this bill had been going on for a decade, and I was familiar with most of it, but I wasn't familiar with the live television procedure for covering such a debate. First of all, Skip explained, the photographer and I would videotape a portion of the House in session, including "sound bites" from both supporters and critics of the bill. Then, at my direction, a tape editor would cut a minute-long videotape track of the representatives debating, followed by back-to-back sound bites from the two sides. I would introduce the piece live on camera, "talk over" silent pictures of the House debate for exactly twenty seconds, and pause for the two sound bites. Then I would give a summary of what the representatives had done that day.

"Remember," Skip said, "when you see the videotape start to

roll from the monitor at your feet, talk only for twenty seconds. Otherwise, you'll be talking over your sound bites." Suddenly, this whole business sounded much too complicated. The photographer and I headed for the Capitol.

After fifteen minutes in the House gallery we had plenty of cover tape and sound bites. The bill's sponsors promised to rid the roadside of unsightly beer cans, and their opponents warned of the loss of jobs for the hundreds of "good working men and women" who make or fill aluminum cans. Pretty predictable stuff. We fed the tape via minicam truck back to the station: twenty seconds of silent pictures, a twenty-second sound bite from the bill's author, and a twenty-second sound bite from a critic. That wasn't so tough and it was only three-thirty.

By five o'clock, an hour before my live debut, my stomach started to churn slightly, and my hands became damp. That was nothing compared to the state of my mind and body forty-five minutes later, when they turned the lights on and gave me a tiny transmitter to drape over my ear so I could hear the anchorman Dave Moore. Suddenly I couldn't remember how I was going to introduce the issue. Notes were no good for this portion, I'd been told, because eye contact with the camera was essential.

"You're just talking directly to the camera as though it were a longtime personal friend," Skip had said. Yeah, well, I had never talked to friends while standing in front of spotlights, holding a microphone, wearing an earpiece, and glancing out of the corner of my eye at a television set at my feet. At five minutes to six, I'd managed to pull myself more or less together: I could remember my name and parts of the introduction I'd written.

"Meanwhile at the Minnesota legislature," Dave Moore was telling the audience, "the House took up debate on a bill its supporters say would save resources and help clean up the state roadsides. Here's reporter Dave Nimmer with more on the story."

Too late for any second thoughts: I was on the air.

"Well, Dave," I began, "the debate over the mandatory-deposit bill is not new in these legislative halls. And neither is the issue, which pits environmentalists against organized labor."

I was rolling now, occasionally glancing at my notes and recalling with ease the facts and figures I'd jotted down. And then in my earpiece I heard someone say, "The videotape is rolling."

I glanced at the monitor at my feet, and there were the pictures of the representatives on the House floor. At this point, for some unknown reason, I stopped talking and tossed my notes on the floor, as though I were through. However, the airwaves were transmitting silent pictures, no sound, and no reporter describing what was happening. The photographer whispered, "Say something, say anything." I retrieved my jumbled notes from the floor.

"So in conclusion," I intoned, "it was the same old arguments with the same old result." I stopped. That was my summary, but we were still in the middle of my live shot. I started to ad lib—no, babble—while all the time hearing another voice in my ear and then another. I was now talking over those sound bites of the representative and his critic.

By the time the shot came back to me at the Capitol, I'd made an idiot out of myself in front of a quarter of a million people. The videotape showed beads of sweat rolling down my forehead and cheeks. I stammered to a close. "Dave," I said, "it doesn't appear likely that the House will pass the bill, at least not this year. For the moment, the issue is dead."

And so, I thought, was my fledgling television career. The photographer packed his camera and lights quickly and left without looking at me or asking if I wanted a ride. I took a taxi back to the station, wondering what people would say and what I would say in return.

When I walked into the basement studio in Minneapolis, the news director Ron Handberg, an old friend and the guy who had hired me, put a hand on my shoulder and said, "You can say one thing about that live shot—it took a lot of guts to be still standing there at the end."

There is another thing you can say about it: in the news business there's always tomorrow and another story and another chance.

A Wounded Eagle

The idea belonged to the photographer Gordie Bartusch, who'd suffered through my rookie jitters at WCCO Television. Now years later, Gordie and I were working together to produce longer stories with a more leisurely pace. Gordie suggested doing a story about a wounded eagle and its treatment at the University of Minnesota Raptor Center.

The folks at the raptor center would call us when a bird was coming, and we would follow that bird through its recovery until its release.

Several weeks had passed, and I'd forgotten the idea in the rush of news stories. Then Gordie came running up to my desk. "They got an eagle from somewhere out in the Dakotas," he said. "She's apparently been shot and got a broken wing and some other damage." Gordie was at the airport for the arrival of the crate containing one very scared and bedraggled bald eagle.

As the weeks passed, Gordie took some remarkable pictures of the bird in her crate, the X-rays of her broken wing, and the patient and persistent efforts to coax her to eat. But this was mostly Gordie's project. My attention was on other stories, until the raptor center phoned that the eagle was ready for release. Would I like to be the one to set her free?

Even as we headed out to the bluffs overlooking the Saint Croix River on that February morning, I was pretty blasé. It was a fine morning on the Saint Croix bluffs south of the Twin Cities, warm for February, and I could feel the sun's luscious heat on my cheeks. The burr oaks still had their brown leaves, and the snow out in the country was still white, glistening in the sun.

A dozen people were standing around at the bluff, staff from the raptor center, a few interested bystanders, and three of us from WCCO. Gordie had arranged for another photographer in case he missed the shot when the eagle flew. Then they brought the eagle to me. The bird was struggling, and I wondered whether I'd be able to hold onto this feathered time bomb. The raptor-center technicians told me to hold the bird on its back, firmly grasping its feet, and then to throw it into the air.

Once I got the bird, she was suddenly still, silent, nestled in the crook of my arm. My God, I thought, she's huge, and look at those big, golden, intelligent eyes. I just stared at her, at that powerful beak, those magnificent brown and white feathers, and most of all, those eyes. I swear she knew I was going to let her go.

Gordie interrupted my reverie. "We're ready, any time you want."

"Okay, old girl," I said as the videotape rolled, "this is your moment. Go catch yourself a fish."

I threw her skyward. I remember what followed as though it were in slow motion. Her body turned as she righted herself. Her wings extended, the feathers separating delicately at their tips, and they beat downward and then up and then down again. They looked six feet across, pushing her up and away with the most beautiful and most awesome power I'd ever seen.

She flew above the oaks, still climbing, and then over the river and out of sight. I could still see the look in her eyes. I can see it even now.

Musk Ox

There's nothing like a small bush plane and a thousand square miles of Canadian wilderness beneath its wings to make you aware of your mortality. Dick Nordling and I were in a small Cessna flying down the Thelon River in the middle of the Barrenland Tundra in the Northwest Territories. The pilot was Tom Faess, a guide and camp owner. He had a cigarette in his mouth and a map on his lap. I couldn't see how he could spot a landmark: there was the river, but the rest of the country was a carpet of muskeg, a maze of lakes, and a series of eskers, giant dunes of the sand pushed ahead and left behind by the glaciers. Go down in here, I thought, and we'll never get out alive. I couldn't understand how Dick could be dozing in the back seat.

Dick and I had persuaded our bosses in the WCCO newsroom to bankroll this trip to the Northwest Territories. The author Dan Gapen had asked for company and someone to share expenses. So here we were, heading north out of our base camp at Lynx Lake, to look for a herd of musk ox that were supposedly roaming a small island at the southern edge of Dubawnt Lake. Faess, who owned and operated the Lynx Lake camp, had heard about the musk ox from a fellow bush pilot. He explained that it was hard to spot these shaggy creatures, which look something like buffaloes in overcoats.

He tilted the Cessna on her side to give us our first view of Dubawnt Lake, stretching to the horizon and beyond. I shook Dick's shoulder and pointed at the lake and muttered something about a wild-goose chase. Tom put the little plane "down on the deck" for a closer look and issued a simple set of instructions: "Look for movement. Look for dark spots on those islands." I could see only a blur of water and bog and rock.

The Journey Goes On

"There," Tom said, pointing over his shoulder. "Look down there. Those are musk ox." He began a slow easy circle.

At first they looked like big brown rocks. Then I saw one move—and then another and another. My heart raced, and I let out a whoop: "Musk ox!"

Tom set the pontoons down on the downwind side of the island. He steered into a small rocky cove, and we jumped out. Tom tied the plane to a small bush. Apprehensive, I checked the knot and the rope.

Getting close to the musk ox was not easy. We were two miles downwind, two miles of muskeg, rock, and brambles. I carried the tripod, Dick carried the camera, and Tom scouted ahead. Hiking on muskeg, you can step on a hummock and sink in up to your knee. It was a grunting, groaning, sweating, straining walk, up and down, over and around. Whenever we found high ground, I usually stumbled over a rock. With my free hand I swatted the blackflies biting my ears and neck and forehead. I was about to suggest taking a break when Tom motioned for Dick and me to stop. He was lying at the top of a small ridge, peering over the edge.

"They're right down below," he whispered. "There may be eighteen or twenty of them. They look like they're grazing."

Dick scrambled ahead of me, crouched down, and set up the tripod and camera. He took pictures for several minutes and then motioned for me to come and look. I crawled up beside him, holding my breath. I took my hat off and looked over the edge.

The musk ox seemed prehistoric. They were smaller than I'd expected: almost delicate with their graceful curved horns, dark brown coats, and light brown muzzles. Their eyes made them appear gentle and serene. We watched the herd for almost a half hour, hardly noticing the blackflies. The bulls and the cows stood in a loosely arranged circle around the calves. They would graze on the tundra lichens awhile, then pause, look up, and chew their cud. When we had enough pictures, Tom suggested that I walk over the ridge and come up behind the herd, to see what they'd do.

The Journey Goes On

Down on the same plain, I walked very slowly to within a hundred yards, and they still stood watching me. Then I moved too close for comfort, and they bolted, in full gallop within a second or two. A quarter of a mile away, they stopped and looked back at me. I hoped I was the last human being they would ever see.

The Hunt for Yankee Girl

About a half hour before daybreak Keith Brown and I boarded the *Sea Verse* in Honolulu harbor. This old forty-two-foot diesel charter fishing boat was nicked and scraped on the hull and stained with dried blood and fish scales on the deck, but, we weren't interested in comfort or appearance, and the *Sea Verse* was the only available boat in port. We were there to report on the arrival of Gerry Spiess, the Minnesotan who was sailing his ten-foot boat the *Yankee Girl* across the Pacific from Santa Barbara. He was about to arrive in Hawaii to stay several weeks before continuing to Australia.

Photographer Brown and I wanted to videotape Spiess at sea, but we hadn't mentioned that to the captain of the *Sea Verse*. Pulling out of Honolulu harbor at dawn, he asked us what we'd like to fish for. We weren't planning on fishing, we explained. We wanted to hunt for a ten-foot sailboat whose last known location was just off the coast of Molakai. We wanted to take some pictures and then rush back to the harbor for our satellite-transmission time to Minnesota.

"Jesus," the captain exclaimed, "why can't I get a couple of guys who just want to go fishing?"

The lights in Honolulu and Waikiki Beach twinkled as we moved down the coast, past Diamondhead and out into the channel between Oahu and Molakai.

"Say," said our captain, "can you guys handle the ocean? This strait here has some of the heaviest seas in the world."

"Don't worry about us. We've been on water all our lives." What we didn't know was that there are Minnesota lakes and then there are oceans.

Twenty minutes past Diamondhead, the ocean was knocking

the living daylights, or at least breakfast, out of Keith and me. Some of the swells were eight feet high. The boat would climb up one side and slide down the other, and when it was in a trough, we couldn't see the horizon. Keith was the hanging over the gunwales, making horrible retching sounds and throwing up everything but his socks. I think that's what made me queasy.

Keith settled on a bunk while I tried the shortwave radio. We knew Spiess's frequency and we were probably within ten or fifteen miles of him.

"*Yankee Girl, Yankee Girl.* This is *Sea Verse.* Come in, *Yankee Girl.*" The only reply was static. I kept at these periodic transmissions for about twenty minutes and was about to give up when ever so faintly I heard something.

"*Sea Verse*, this is *Yankee Girl.*"

For the next few minutes Spiess and I talked about where he was and where we were and when we would meet. He apologized for not answering my call earlier: he had heard it but was engaged in his "morning toilet."

I'd last talked to Spiess a month before, when Keith and I were covering his departure in Santa Barbara. And now we were in the middle of the ocean, just a few miles from the halfway point in his journey. Using only a sextant, Spiess knew precisely where he was. He figured we'd meet in about an hour.

Keith began fiddling with his gear. He was going to shoot this story even if someone had to lash him to the mast.

For the next half hour, we kept peering out to sea, looking for a speck on the horizon. Our captain spotted the tip of the mast. "Over there," he said, swinging the binoculars, "about three o'clock."

Keith and I couldn't see anything at first, but soon we could make out a little black speck against the blue of the Pacific. In another ten minutes we could see that it was a boat, bobbing like a little green cork.

"I wouldn't sail that thing across Mille Lacs," I said. "He's got some kind of nerve."

And, indeed, nerve is what Gerry Spiess had. He had been at sea for twenty-eight days, most of them out of contact with another human being. His craft was hardly longer than a bath tub, and yet he had survived wind and rain and at least one full-blown storm.

By the time we got within a quarter of a mile of the *Yankee Girl*, we were talking back and forth constantly on the radio, with perfect transmission. Finally we could see Spiess, wearing a sparkling pair of white shorts with a leg draped over the tiller. He looked as if he were out for a Sunday sail on Lake Minnetonka.

Our diesel craft almost swamped the *Yankee Girl* as we pulled alongside. Spiess deftly maneuvered out of harm's way. He was exuberant. And why not? The sky was blue. The wind was fresh. And the *Yankee Girl*, with a stiff following breeze, was skimming along.

By this time we were approaching Diamondhead, and Keith was capturing on videotape Spiess's sweet moment of triumph and joy. One of the pleasures and privileges of being a reporter is to share other people's moments. How else can you do that and still put in for expenses?

A Pair of Haircuts

The photographer Dick Nordling and I strolled toward the midway at the State Fairgrounds, hoping to find some activity—roustabouts setting up the Tilt-a-Whirl or a kid putting the giant stuffed animals on the shelf at the shooting gallery. We were doing the usual getting-ready-for-the-State-Fair story. We both liked the fair, but it was hard to find anything new to report. Dick had already videotaped a few scenes: two young women scrubbing down the counters at a church food stand and an implement salesman polishing the fender of one of his hundred-thousand-dollar tractors on Machinery Hill. We needed something a little more spectacular—or at least a little different. But on this cool and gray morning the midway was quiet. We were about to head for the livestock barns when a neatly dressed man in his fifties came bustling toward us.

"Taking pictures, huh?" he said. Dick nodded, and I explained our assignment. The man smiled. "Well, speaking of getting ready for the opening, I got a few things to do. Do you know where my sons could get a haircut around here?" We said there was a barber shop within a short drive. He thanked us and then wondered aloud how he'd find the shops, since he wasn't from the Twin Cities. He asked us whether we could drive his sons to the barber, and he added, "You might even be able to get some pictures for your story."

Right. I could hear the ten-o'clock news tease: Boys Get Haircuts As They Prepare for the Opening of the State Fair. He beckoned us to follow, and Dick and I tagged along to his huge semitrailer with a plexiglass window that took up about a third of one side next to a gaudy billboard: "See the world's oldest living Siamese twins—Ronnie and Donnie. Look at them. Talk with them."

The Journey Goes On

The sign described the twins as joined at the abdomen, qualifying as "a genuine medical miracle." I was a little uneasy as I stepped up into the trailer and through the cramped kitchen and into the living room with its couch and shag carpet. The wall opposite the couch was the plexiglass window, where fairgoers could gawk at Ronnie and Donnie.

They got up from the couch as Dick and I walked in. They were both wearing short-sleeved shirts. They were nice-looking young men, probably in their early twenties. Their handshakes were strong and engaging. As they returned to the couch, I noticed they walked sideways, crablike.

They told us their lives had been productive and useful and they were generally happy. They had different tastes and interests—they cheered for different football and baseball teams—but if one caught a cold, the other got it. They couldn't be separated: dozens of doctors had said that was impossible. They lived their lives as normally as they could. They went hunting, swimming, and fishing, but they didn't go out in public much. It was too big a hassle with too many questions, too many obstacles, too many gawkers. So how could they be part of a midway sideshow? It was the only way, they said, to support themselves. If people were going to stare anyway, well, they might as well be paid for it. There were other questions I never asked: How did they manage to use the toilet? Did they ever have girlfriends? Did they want to? Such questions seemed too sensitive for a minute-and-a-half feature on the State Fair.

Dick took a few pictures, but he didn't photograph the twins as they crab-walked to the car and maneuvered into the back seat, where one lay on top of the other. They looked cramped and uncomfortable, but they chatted with us nonstop all the way down Snelling Avenue to the barber shop.

I asked the barber, "Could you give a couple of haircuts and let us take a few pictures while you're doing it?" He said yes, so I dropped the other shoe. "The haircuts," I deadpanned, "are for Siamese twins in the sideshow at the State Fair." The barber didn't blink and never cracked a smile, but he did stare for a moment when I came back with Ronnie and Donnie. He pulled out a pair of stools for the twins. For a while the barber clipped nervously and silently. But as Ronnie and Donnie began chatting with each other, he joined in and soon all three were talking, ignoring Dick and his camera. The haircuts took about twenty minutes each, and I don't remember who paid. Ronnie and Donnie each liked his haircut.

As I was about to get in the car, the barber waved and hollered. I went back to his shop. "You know," he said, "I thought you were shittin' me about the Siamese twins. This was the damnedest thing." This would be something to tell his grandkids about. Then he said it was a little eerie clipping the hair on the back of Donnie's neck while looking into Ronnie's eyes.

On the way back to the fairgounds, the twins asked us about television and how a news show was put together. We explained the basics and asked them if they would like to spend a couple of hours at the station during the Fair. They said they certainly would. We said we'd check it out and get back to them.

That afternoon I wrote my Fair preview, looked at the videotape, and picked out the sound bites. I used a few snippets of Ronnie and Donnie and their haircuts, resisting the temptation to build the entire story around them. Our newsroom colleagues had varied reactions to Dick's and my stories about the twins, ranging from uninterest to morbid curiosity to mild revulsion. "Oh, how gross," said one young producer when I described the twins' crab walk. Dick and I were disappointed by their comments and forgot about inviting the twins to the station. They never called, and a week later the Fair was over. The midway was closed, and they were gone to their next booking, somewhere in the Dakotas, as I recall.

Sometimes I think what a marvelous story it would have made to follow the twins around the country for a summer, to ask the sensitive questions and handle the answers gracefully. I don't know whether Ronnie and Donnie ever returned to the State Fair. I don't go to the midway anymore. These days, the rides are either too slow or too fast, and I've lost my taste for freak shows.

A Damn Good Painter

On the Christmas I met Don and his family, I gave and received the most memorable gifts of my life.

I'd always hated those assignments to cover a shelter or a food shelf and talk to the poor people eating a Thanksgiving or Christmas dinner. It always seemed intrusive and even exploitive. On this Christmas Day the photographer Dick Nordling and I decided to visit the House of Charity—it was close, and I knew the manager. When we arrived, the dining hall was filled with men and women sitting at tables and still wearing their overcoats. It was quiet. Mealtime here was no sociable occasion. It was time to fill your belly, get warm, and get out.

"So who do you want to talk with?" the dining room manager asked.

"Have you got a family, maybe a couple of kids, a mother and a father?"

He pointed to a corner of the room.

"There's a guy over there with his wife and three kids. He seems nice enough. At least he's not likely to tell you to get lost."

I told Dick to stay where he was, and I went over to the man. "Merry Christmas," I said. "I'm a TV reporter, and I'm looking to talk with a family that needs a little help at Christmas."

He told me his name was Don. He and his family had come here from Texas a couple of months ago looking for work. He was a painter, "a damn good one, if I do say so myself." But he couldn't find work, and his monthly welfare payment of two hundred dollars only paid half the rent on a two-bedroom walk-up. "So here I am. I figure at least the kids can enjoy a dinner that makes it seem like Christmas."

His two youngest children, a girl about seven and her brother about six, were happily eating their turkey, dressing, and sweet potatoes. Their older brother had seen Dick's camera and had left the dining hall.

"You'll have to excuse him," Don's wife said. "He didn't want to be here. He's embarrassed."

So was I, but I plunged ahead. Don and his wife agreed to talk and be photographed. I had my story, a troubled family at Christmas.

"Maybe somebody will see it," I said after the interview, "somebody who'll have a painting job for you." I helped Dick pack up his photographic gear, and I was about to say goodbye and be on my way, but before I could think about it, I blurted out, "Say Don, my bathroom at home needs to be papered and painted. Maybe you could do the job."

He put his fork down and said, "You bet. How about Friday?"

"Call me. Here's my number at work. I'm not home during the day, so we'll have to work something out."

"You think about it," Don said, "and I'll call you tomorrow."

All that Christmas Day I thought about it. I'd have to give him the key to my house: it was the only way. And Don didn't come with a long list of references. But I decided to trust my instincts, my judgment, my fellow man.

When Don called the next day, I told him to stop by the television station and pick up the key to my house. I told him to work on the half bathroom: grass paper on the bottom half and a new coat of ivory paint on the top. "You look at the room and pick out the paper," I said, "and I'll write you a check for the materials."

On Friday, I wrote Don a check for seventy-two dollars for paper, paste, brushes, and paint. By then he'd been to the house to look at the bathroom, and so far so good. He'd locked up behind him, and nothing was missing.

That afternoon one of my neighbors phoned me at work. "I just saw the strangest sight," she said. "Some guy got off the bus at the corner with a couple of kids and his wife, I guess. He was carrying a stepladder and some buckets, and they went into your house."

"Oh, yeah," I said, "I should have told you. I hired this guy to paint my bathroom."

"I hope he knows what he's doing. I mean, he doesn't even own a car."

"Don't worry. He comes highly recommended."

That night I roared into the driveway, jumped out of the car, and almost ran into the house.

Inside, on a table I found my key and a short note. Don thanked me for the work, for paying him in advance, and for trusting him. He said he'd bought the kids some Christmas presents.

Then I walked into the bathroom. It looked beautiful. Everything was neat and even. The ivory paint had not a brush mark, the grass paper had not a wrinkle, and the floor had not a speck of paint. Turning back to my problems, my chores, and my life, I forgot about Don and his family, and I never saw them again. And I probably would never have thought of them again, except when I moved from that house a year later as I was cleaning out the drawers, including the ones in the vanity table in that half bathroom, I found a five dollar bill and seventeen cents and a note from Don: "Thanks again, Dave. You paid me too much for the wallpaper."

Part III

The Right Woman

The Right Woman

On the third and last day of our short honeymoon, we were bundled up against the cold as we walked down Chicago's Michigan Avenue, decked out in Christmas ornaments and cluttered with shoppers. Neither of us spoke. I was thinking about being married, really being married, to this woman whose hand was clasped in mine.

My first marriage had been a disaster; we'd lasted barely three years and probably hadn't had a truthful exchange but once or twice. Maybe it was my fault, but I thought it was hers. And until I met Kris, I was convinced I'd never marry again.

Kris had turned out to be a good friend, a fair fighter, and a lovely companion. But as we walked past the Tribune Tower, I still couldn't shake my uneasiness. Did I do the right thing? Can we make it? Do we have enough in common? What don't I know about her? I squeezed her hand, smiled at her, and wondered whether she had the same thoughts. Still, neither of us said a word. We hurried along, as though we had somewhere to go.

We almost bumped into a man in front of a men's shop. He was blind, in his sixties, with a full head of gray hair. The creases in his face seemed to indicate he smiled a lot. He was panhandling with a cup of pencils in his hand. I nudged Kris to move faster, so we could pass him without being accosted.

Several steps past him, Kris stopped. "Hold on," she said. "I've got to go back." I followed her as she walked back to the blind man.

"Here," she said to him, "I want you to have this." She put a five-dollar bill in his hand, folding his fingers around the money.

He smiled and thrust out the cup of pencils. "Take one of

these." Kris thanked him, said she didn't need any pencils, and turned to leave.

"Wait," he said, "I need your opinion. I just got this overcoat today, got it from the Salvation Army, and I'd kind of like to know how it looks."

Kris moved toward him and put her hand on his shoulder. "It looks just fine," she said, "and you look fine wearing it."

He thanked her. Kris turned to walk away. This time she was crying.

This time I had married the right woman.

My French Masterpiece

I hadn't been an eager traveler so far on my first trip to Europe. Paris had been a blur of crowded sidewalks, stifling diesel exhaust fumes, and aging museums. This was a honeymoon of sorts for me and Kris, who finds adventure and bliss in France, but I couldn't seem to find a way to make this my trip too.

There were moments, like standing atop the Eiffel Tower at twilight, struck by the whiteness of the city and the almost mystical emanations from Notre Dame and Sacré Coeur. Or sitting at a little table for breakfast at our hotel, the Sèvres-Azur, eating huge croissants with strawberry jam and sipping café au lait. But for every moment of magic there were two of apprehension and angst. I couldn't find my way around, especially on the tiny side streets. I didn't respond to art, paintings, and sculptures by the masters. And my French was nonexistent, so it was up to Kris to find our way, make all the arrangements, and even order our food. Once while I was mustering the courage to order "deux cafés au lait, s'il vous plaît," Kris—unaware of my effort—jumped in before I could speak. No, this wasn't going well, and I made no secret of it. When Kris remarked on the lovely reflections in the Seine, I retorted that the famous river was dirtier and more polluted than I had expected. She saw mirrored images and I noticed beer bottles.

I was glad when we picked up our rental car and headed southeast into the French countryside. We spent the first night at Auxerre, a charming little town full of bridges and churches. The next morning as we headed for the foothills of the Alps, I began to feel more involved in the trip. I was driving now, proud of myself for following the road signs and negotiating the sharp curves. By midafternoon the countryside was changing as we ascended toward the mountains. Pine forests replaced the farm fields. Rivers were smaller, faster, and cleaner. Wildflowers dotted the meadows. In the tiny towns along the way, chalets stood beside the road, with their shutters and window boxes filled with pink, red, and yellow flowers. Our old graystone hotel at Saint-Claude sat on the bank of a sparkling, churning alpine stream.

As we sipped coffee in a little bar and grill after a good night's sleep, I was excited about driving in the Alps. We were continuing south for Briançon, the country's highest city and the training ground for the French alpine soldiers. The road out of Saint-Claude wasn't wide, but I was driving well, Kris was navigating enthusiastically, and the weather was cooperating with blue skies and a warm breeze. For several hours we headed up and across the Alps, negotiating frequent switchbacks.

In the early evening we chugged to the top of this alpine range, inched our way through the mountain pass, and started down the other side in low gear. There weren't any guardrails or highway markers on this bed of loose shale and small rocks, where the shoulder gave way to thin air and a half mile drop down the mountainside. I had both hands on the wheel, a foot on the brake, and cold sweat in the small of my back. My eyes were glued to the gray shale roadway. As I snaked around a curve, I was relieved to see a small plateau where the road veered away from the cliff edge. I glanced up and around, just in time to see my own French masterpiece.

There was a warm golden haze in the sky as dusk approached, and twenty yards ahead was an old man, carrying a staff, smoking a pipe, wearing a blue beret and jacket, and driving four cows, each with a bell around her neck, across the road to a small stone barn. He moved slowly, seemingly unaware of our presence. It was as though we'd been whisked ten centuries back into the past. When was the barn built? How did this farmer's ancestors get up here? Suddenly we were in an older, less American world. I tried to imagine where Hannibal had prodded his elephants through these Alps and where the French resistance had battled the Germans. As we pulled into Briançon that night, I was pleased with myself. I was discovering how to travel: to feel the history, appreciate the differences, savor the moment.

This élan lasted about twenty-four hours, until we drove from Briançon to the six-lane freeway heading into Nice on the French Riviera. The traffic was horrible, with cars whizzing by left and right. The freeway signs were unintelligible. And I was uncooperative. I pulled over on an emergency shoulder, gave Kris the car keys and told her to drive. She found an exit ramp, and we searched in vain for a hotel. I grumbled and groused at her every suggestion. She smiled, being well past the point of exasperation, and sweetly asked whether I had any good ideas.

That night we stayed at a Holiday Inn.

In the Mountains

I had never hiked in the mountains, but in the years between my marriages an old friend, Jim Shoop, talked me into joining him, his wife Pris, and two of their kids, David and Nancy, on a vacation to Glacier National Park. Deborah Howell, my editor friend from the *Saint Paul Pioneer Press*, went along too, since she had already hiked in the Grand Tetons. All the way out in our rented camper—across the North Dakota prairie and the rolling wheatland of northern Montana—I just couldn't understand my companions' enthusiasm, not even when we rolled into the Two Medicine campground, where I had my first close-up look at the Rockies. They were beautiful all right, but they belonged to a picture postcard, with their intriguing names—Pinnacle Wall, Lone Walker, Sinopah.

The next morning we hiked to Scenic Point, atop a small mountain overlooking Upper Two Medicine Lake. We started through a stand of shrubs and lodgepole pines on the way to the trailhead. I looked up and thought, this is bigger than it looked from the campground. Up we started. I was concentrating on the trail to avoid spraining an ankle on my first mountain hike. For several hundred yards the trail wound lazily up the mountainside. I wasn't even breathing hard yet.

Fifteen minutes later, mouth open, I was sucking for air as I followed the Shoop's son David up a series of switchbacks. Until that morning I never heard of the term for these zigzag paths across the face of the mountain. I'd walked three or four of them before I had to stop and rest. For the first time I looked around and down at the tumbling glacial river in the valley below, the wind-whipped turquoise waters of Two Medicine, and the straight gray skeletons of the dead fir trees on the mountainside below.

Now I was becoming part of the country around me. Suddenly there were secrets to discover, like the pine shrubs, whose roots grab at the rocky ground, and the wildflowers, the delicate yellow buttercup and the brilliant red Indian paintbrush.

I started to walk again, faster and faster, to climb higher for another view of the snowfield on the mountain across from us and the tiny waterfall that seemed to spurt out of the red rock wall ahead. I was amazed by my stamina, my quick stride and strong step. I was only a few strides behind David when we reached the mountain saddle at Scenic Point. The wind, strong and chill, whistled past my ears. With an exhilaration I'd never known before, I felt as though I had climbed to the top of the world.

All our hikes added another memory, another intimacy with the mountains of Glacier. At Iceberg Lake sheets of ice and snow fell from the mountain slopes into its bright blue waters. On the climb to Sperry Chalet I glimpsed a distant stone lodge that appeared to be balancing on one of the cliffs. It was from a childhood dream of a Tibetan monastery or a lost city. That evening Deborah and David and I climbed to a peak above the chalet and looked down on our mountain meadow and Lake McDonald. The air was warm and the sky had a golden hue, enveloping everything with a soft delicacy. We just stood there, silent, peaceful, and grateful.

I came back from that trip with a new passion, a key to unlock some of the doors and gates on my spiritual journey. But, as with other keys, I misplaced this one temporarily. I found it a few years later, after I'd married Kris. She has a way of moving me along life's journey, sometimes with a hip shot but usually with a subtle nudge. When Kris suggested we take a trip out West to find a place we could share with equal enthusiasm, she mentioned Yellowstone. I said Glacier. We agreed on both.

Glacier was our first stop, and with my penchant for trying to control situations and people around me, I was apprehensive as I turned the car off the highway and down the road to the Swift Current campground. Kris had seen the mountains of Glacier a few years back, and she allowed as how they were nice, "but they didn't make me crazy." Would she share my passion for these mountains? Would she feel what I felt? Would I feel the same way again?

As we strapped on our day packs and set off on the trail to Iceberg Lake, I silently vowed to let the high country do the persuading. We climbed for about a half mile past a hillside covered with the soft green leaves of the thistleberry shrubs, through a stand of small fir trees, and up onto the mountain trail. The sky was cloudless, the sun felt warm, and the breeze was cool enough to take the sweat from our brows.

"David, hold on a minute." I stopped and turned back. Kris was looking at the valley behind us. "This is simply magnificent," she said. "It's all so huge. I just never dreamed"—I hugged her.

When we reached the lake, we sat on a rock and looked at the bear grass on the meadow behind us, and the snow-covered mountain amphitheater in front of us. The rocks in the water at our feet were colored peach, pink, and mauve. We shared a can of soda, a muffin and an apple for lunch. We listened to the wind whistling around the mountain cliffs. We flopped on our backs and let the sun warm us. We told each other how lucky we were.

Some of our mountain moments, though, were less than spiritual. For instance, on our hike up to Iceberg Lake, Kris had periodically reminded me that we didn't have any bear bells on our packs. She'd been told to make noise on the trail to avoid surprising any grizzly sow with her cubs. I explained that the bells don't make much noise and that probably no bear had crossed the trail for weeks. Quit worrying, I told her. Then on our hike down from Iceberg Lake we came upon a dozen hikers clustered together at a bend in the trail. Just moments before, they'd met a bear that fortunately was more interested in fleeing that fighting. "No bears to worry about, huh?" said Kris. We bought bear bells the following morning.

Dozens of other creatures, large and small, have crossed paths with me and Kris. We found a fat and sassy pair of marmots midway through their change from winter white to summer tan. They were scrapping over a delicate root. While one was chewing away, the other was nipping at his fanny. He'd turn and chatter and resume his meal. Eventually his tormentor left.

The Journey Goes On

On a hike up to Old Man Lake we spied a tiny green frog. The summer had been dry, and the creek beds were stone and dust with sometimes a trickle of water. The lime-green frog, no bigger than a quarter, looked delicate, even frail. I knelt beside him and he didn't move. "What are you going to do, fella, if this creek dries up?" The nearest creek was a mile away.

On our way down the mountain we watched a golden eagle soar, riding the thermal currents. She would beat her wings once or twice and then catch a warm draft. Up she would go two hundred yards. Then she would veer down and do it over again. Finally she rose up and up against the mountain wall, over the rim and out of sight.

We never made it to Yellowstone, partly because of the fires there that year, but mostly because we were reluctant to leave Glacier. Someday maybe we'll make it to Yellowstone, but meanwhile we have returned to Glacier.

We tested our endurance, our courage, and our common sense on a hike to Crypt Lake on the Canadian side of the park. For the first four miles our hike was easy, through familiar terrain. We were following Hell Roaring Creek, and every now and then we caught a breath-taking glimpse of the falls tumbling a quarter of a mile down the mountainside. We struggled up the switchbacks of the final mile to climb to the source of that waterfall: tiny Crypt Lake, just behind the mountain ridge. Good Lord, I thought, there's hardly a trace of a trail across the cliff.

The trail went through the cliff, through a small tunnel, which we reached by climbing an iron ladder hanging from the ledge above. Those were the longest seven steps of my life, one rung at a time. "Now let go of the ladder. Grab that rock. Swing your foot up. Good. Now the other." I was talking to myself in that old one-step-at-a-time approach that seems to ease the panic. In the tunnel, crawling into the darkness ahead, my knees were stiff, and my hips wouldn't move, and the backpack kept catching on the jutting rocks. The ten yards seemed like ten miles.

At the other end the mountain had disappeared! I was staring into space. I peeked over the edge and saw the trail below. It wasn't more than eight inches wide and covered with loose rock.

"Now, just ease on down. Put your feet on the trail," I said to myself. With my left hand I grabbed a cable spiked into the rock. I put my right foot forward and brought up my left. Damn, I thought, this is crazy. But I made it. Kris arrived, overcoming a slight case of panic. She was angry at herself for attempting such a stupid stunt. As we climbed the last few feet together, I thought about the difference of our reactions: my triumph, her folly.

When we saw the lake, however, our response was singular. It was beautiful. A huge sheet of ice was still floating in the middle. The mountain bowl above and around it was etched in snow, but the meadow in front of it was alive with spring greenery in the middle of July—the reddish-pink of the alpine laurel, the bright yellow of the shrubby cinquefoil, and the delicate ivory of the cascade mountain ash. Trout were dappling the lake's unfrozen surface, feeding on a new insect hatch.

Hiking in the mountains, one has a sense of perfection or at least of the exquisite way the pieces fit together in nature's puzzle. Once a cow elk crossed our path on a hike to Siyeh Pass. Unafraid, she walked to about ten feet from us, arching her powerful neck to inspect these two-legged interlopers. And the mountain goats in the meadow near Hidden Lake grazed contentedly as we walked up and snapped pictures. They seemed to understand that we meant them no harm. They were dining on glacier lilies, tiny meadow plants with delicate yellow flowers. These lilies typify the hardy determination of life in the high country. As we crossed the snowpack that still covered parts of the meadow, we could see their slender green shoots poking through. How did they know it was time to sprout? How could they break through a half foot of ice and snow?

Near the end of one of our hikes, I was swinging along at a pretty good pace. "David," Kris said. I stopped and looked back. "I just hope that 25 years from now we'll be on some mountain trail, and I'll be looking at your backside up ahead."

I thanked her. I thought, God, let me be there. I don't even have to be in the lead.

Waiting for the Train

At eight o'clock the July evening was cool, especially compared to the near-hundred degree temperatures we had left behind in the Twin Cities. Kris and I were standing on the old brick platform in front of the train station at Montana's East Glacier. I had persuaded her to join me at the depot to watch the evening passenger train, the Empire Builder, come rumbling off the high prairie and stop at the little station. I hadn't watched a train pull in for thirty years. As a kid, I loved trains—the smell of diesel fuel, the sound of the whistle, the heart-pounding rumble of the engine.

Like something designed by Walt Disney, this depot of logs and huge timbers fronts the tiny town of East Glacier. Across the shiny steel tracks were the Conoco station, the neon-lighted Park Bar, P. J.'s Motel and Diner, and the painted wooden sign of the Whistling Swan Motel. The main street was deserted except for a cowboy tinkering with the engine of his pickup truck. His boots were worn and dusty, his hat was soiled and bent, and a couple of well-worn saddles lay in the bed of his truck. To the east the sunlight was shimmering on the green prairie grass in the distance, and to the west the patches of snow on the mountain tops glistened.

The train was already half an hour late, but the dozen people standing around didn't seem to mind. A couple of college kids, their backpacks resting against their knees, were sitting on a bench. A middle-aged man, wearing a Chicago Bear's jacket, was taking pictures. And three little children, with straight black hair and large dark eyes, were running alongside the tracks, pointing and giggling. They were probably from the Blackfoot Indian reservation bordering the park. While waiting, I took in all the details:

the depot's flower boxes with marigolds and petunias and snap dragons and even a couple of tomato plants, the old green baggage cart with its red spoke wheels next to the tracks and laden with suitcases and boxes, and the station manager with his bristly red beard, as he cautioned everyone not to track dirt and tar onto his freshly scrubbed depot floor.

The ticket agent, a sprightly woman in her late forties, had an easy smile. I asked her about last winter's snowfall, and she launched into a yarn about the day she had to climb over a five-foot drift to reach the depot door, only to find it wouldn't open because the hinges were frozen. Someone asked her about a rumor that an Ohio couple had been mauled by a black bear.

"Oh, yes," she said, "they were coming down from Avalanche Lake. The wind was blowing so hard the bear couldn't see them or smell them. She had a cub and apparently got surprised. She took after the wife first, and when the husband took after her with a stick, she chewed on him. It was just one of those things. But at least they're both alive—took 'em by helicopter to the hospital in Kalispell."

Then we heard a distant noise to the east. It was more like a horn than a whistle. "The train, Mommy, the train," squealed one of the kids. I grabbed Kris by the hand and ran down the platform to see the headlight and the silver cars as they rounded the curve onto the straightaway into the depot.

As the engine passed us, the engineer opened the window of his cab and waved to the kids, and the baggage car, the coach cars, and the dining car rolled by. When the train stopped, I was standing in front of the sleeper car, which had two levels or stories or whatever you call them on a train. Its door slid open, and out stepped the conductor, a woman. Half a dozen passengers got on, while twice as many got off—kids with their backpacks, middle-aged couples with their suitcases, and a fisherman with his fly rod.

They made their way past the five or six local business people with their homemade signs: "Need a Car? Rent a Wreck." "Try P. J.'s Motel—Just 1 Block East."

By then the train had been there fifteen minutes. Three conductors were standing on the platform: the woman in front of me,

The Journey Goes On

one way down at the end of the train, and just behind the engine, one who was nervously checking his pocket watch, like the watch my grandfather used to pull out of that odd little pocket in his trousers. The conductor hollered, "Board!" The engineer gave a short blast on the horn, and all three conductors stepped up into their coaches and shut the doors. The train started to move, slowly at first and then faster and faster. Suddenly the last car had rolled past me.

She pulled away from the station, toward the mountains to the west. It was half an hour before dusk and the sky was still a bright blue, with the sun's rays reflecting off the last car. I shaded my eyes with my hands to see her disappear around a curve. "She's on her way to Seattle," I said softly.

My heart was pounding, just the way it did when I was fourteen.

Becker the Cat

Becker was a small black and white cat, with crossed eyes. He used to roam the ditches, fields, and marshes near our old farmhouse. Even at twenty below zero, we'd see him running lickety-split along the road or across a field.

Kris and I speculated that he was a wild cat who had to hunt for food. In the winter, he'd check the base of our bird feeder for pieces of fruit and suet among the seeds. Somehow he survived from year to year.

One spring he began hanging around at the edge of our yard. From time to time when we were on the deck, he'd edge up to within ten yards of us. He always raced away if we made the slightest move toward him.

Then one warm Saturday morning as Kris was about to go jogging, she whispered, "David, come look." I tiptoed to the patio door. There, curled up on one of the patio chairs, was the cat, sound asleep. "I'm going to leave a little cat food out for him," Kris said.

For several days she set out some of our own cat's food in the evening and took it back in every morning. But one morning the plate was empty. The next evening the little cat ventured back onto our deck for the dry Kibbles. He'd eat a mouthful, look around warily, eat another mouthful, and look around again.

Within a week, Kris had named the cat Becker, after the psychologist and philosopher Ernest Becker. By then Becker would come up on the deck to eat in front of us, still watchful, however. He followed a routine, arriving about seven in the evening, eating his meal in two sittings, taking a drink of water, and wandering off. Kris made a couple of attempts to pet him, and each time he bolted. One night, however, he let Kris to scratch him behind the

The Journey Goes On

ears. "It feels like such an honor," she said, "as though he's allowing us to share a tiny bit of his life. And it must have been a hard one."

Soon he would eat and then approach so Kris could rub his back and scratch his ears. He became aggressive about getting this attention, as though he had just discovered affection and couldn't get enough. One night he even allowed me to pet him. His body was like a coiled spring, tough and sinewy. The little guy had had to hustle to stay alive. We were wondering if we knew a family to take care of him.

Then one day Kris phoned me at work. "Come home and help me. Becker bit me on the arm. I need to catch him and take him to the vet." He had sunk his four sharpest teeth in her forearm. "It wasn't his fault," she said. "He got scared by our cat at the patio door and just reacted." We caught him without the slightest struggle and Kris took him to the vet, where he was neutered and given a rabies shot. He was quarantined at the local humane society, to see whether he'd develop rabies symptoms. That night at supper Kris hardly spoke. "I feel so bad that Becker is now in a cage. That's all because of us."

Ten days later Kris picked up the cat, and we decided that Becker belonged outdoors, but by now he was more like our pet than a wild cat. He showed up on the deck at all hours during the day. As we did chores in the yard, he followed us around and insisted on being stroked and scratched. Becker had adopted us. Meanwhile, Kris was running through a list of friends for someone who might gamble on taking Becker.

One night Becker's instincts overtook him again. When I moved too suddenly to go indoors after petting him, Becker bit me on the ankle, as if to say, "No, not yet, don't go in yet." But his bite drew blood. Now we knew that Becker couldn't be a house pet, and thanks to us, he couldn't be wild again either.

"We'll have to have him put down," Kris said. "What's so hard is that there aren't any choices. And what's harder is that it's not his fault."

I told Kris I'd catch Becker. She said she wanted to be the one to take him to the vet in the morning. I didn't argue. That night I sat on the deck, and Becker came and demanded to be petted.

"Well, old boy," I said, "I think this is it." I held open the door to a plastic travel cage, and he walked right in. "You shouldn't have done that, Becker," I said. "You should have highballed it out of here. You should never have trusted us in the first place."

I put the cage in the garage and shut the door before I could hear Becker cry. The next morning Kris took Becker to the vet. She phoned me when it was over. That night when I got home, I went out to sit on the deck and stare at Becker's empty little food plate.

North Shore Rituals

Kris and I know precisely when the North Shore experience starts: two and a half miles south of Duluth on Interstate 35. The car reaches the crest of the ridge, and I open the window and stick my hand out to feel that crisp cool air. We look down on the city, the backwaters of the Saint Louis River, the smokestacks of the paper mill, the two-story clapboard houses on the hillsides, the aerial-lift bridge and the blue expanse of Lake Superior in the distance.

It's always a welcome signal to mind and body to downshift a couple of gears. I've always liked Duluth. It strikes me as an honest, hard-working town, with grit and grime and shoulders. Duluth is a barrel-chested kind of town, though its character changes on the North Shore drive past Glensheen and the well-kept mansions with their terraced lawns and flower gardens.

Once over the Lester River, we never stop until Two Harbors, perhaps for a quick trip to the supermarket for a box of cereal or a head of lettuce. Then we're back on Highway 61 and the rhythm of its curves, hills, narrow shoulders, and scenic overlooks. This is a highway for driving and watching, not cruising. The landmarks and road signs are like old friends: the traffic lights at Silver Bay, the missionary Father Baraga's Cross, the birch trees on the hillsides of the Sawtooth range near Tofte and the Lutsen Resort sign that used to advertise the fresh pie of the day.

Lutsen reminds us to watch for the sign tucked among the poplars and pines along the roadside: Spruce Creek. We make a quick right turn, and soon we're pulling up to the front door of Hillside, our cabin on the creek.

We always unload the car as fast as we can. Cooler, clothes, coffeepot—we've got them unpacked, hung up, or tucked away in fifteen minutes. Then I look out the kitchen's picture window at that same little bay, that same wall of granite, that same tumbling tiny creek. No matter what mischief or mayhem has intruded on our lives in the past year, the same colors and shapes and sounds and smells wait for us.

There's a routine for the first night and every day that follows. It begins with building a fire, Kris reading a book, and me writing at the kitchen table until I get too tired to concentrate and I pick up a book of my own. And before we turn in, we check the sky, look for stars, catch a breeze, and speculate about tomorrow's weather.

In the morning while Kris is jogging, I drive to the general store for the Twin Cities newspapers. Usually, I have Highway 61 to myself. I notice a new Native American art gallery in a cedar cabin. There's the True Value Hardware store and the Lutheran Church. And there's the general store. I like shopping in an establishment that sells bacon, crackers, milk, and fishing tackle. It's comforting to know that you can get a dozen minnows with your *Star Tribune*. Although I never mention it to my male fishing buddies, I eat mostly healthy food when I'm on the North Shore, stuff like high-fiber cereal and fresh lake trout with ground pepper, lemon, onion, and only a touch of salt.

The lake trout I buy in Grand Marais on another trip. You have to arrive at the store at the right time, when one of the few remaining commercial fishermen brings in fresh fillets. On my way back, there's always time to stop at the Ben Franklin Store to check the shelves and think whether I need wool socks or boot polish or a plaid flannel shirt.

Grand Marais is also a good place to see how fishermen are outfitted these days—what they're wearing, carrying, casting or towing—since the town is the gateway to the resorts on the Gunflint Trail and to the Boundary Waters Canoe Area. I can look for the latest in backpacking equipment, V-hull boats and campers. At the high-class outfitters you can spot the northwoods tenderfeet, wearing their paisley shorts and pink sunglasses, perhaps about to run into their first swarm of blackflies or their first attempt to pitch a tent in a rainstorm.

The Journey Goes On

On the way back to the cabin I'm always grateful we have hot water and ice cubes. But we aren't sedentary on the shore: we hike down northwoods roads, over tiny creeks, past old cedars and young pine seedlings. There, in a meadow, is a batch of purple lupine. And over there, on the other side of the road, are the tiny white blossoms of the wild strawberries.

Sometimes we walk to supper about three miles down the road to a little restaurant at the mouth of the Cascade River. I can stand on a rock there for hours, casting my fishing spoons into the eddies, where the river's current meets the waters of Lake Superior. Once in a while I even get a strike and feel again the throb of a lake trout. People who fish with a quarter of pound of lead or wire line ought to feel the trout's power and energy on light line and tackle. I confess: I've never landed one of these lakers. And the cast-to-strike ratio must be five hundred to one. But a fisherman can watch the cartwheeling gulls, a newly hatched swarm of dragonflies, and school after school of tiny lake-trout fry darting in and out among the rocks. There's always enough of a breeze to keep the mosquitoes from your neck or the sweat from your brow.

The North Shore is full of these moments. It seems indestructible, yet its ecosystem is fragile. It seems hospitable, yet I know its sting in November. And the lake seems immense, yet I can sense its soul. The lake and the shore never fail to set my spirit soaring, yet I never feel more vulnerable than when I am there. I relish the privacy and solitude, yet I never love Kris as much. The North Shore is a vital part of our lives. With care and luck, it will be there for others, long after we're gone.

Part IV

The Formula

The Formula

By six in the morning the day already felt hot—no breeze, no clouds. The air, as my grandmother used to say, was so heavy you could cut it with a knife. My fishing buddy Tom Mihokanich came out on the deck with fresh coffee. We were staying at a friend's cabin on Minnesota's Iron Range to explore the pothole bass lakes. This morning we planned to prowl for bass on a little lake we'd discovered the night before.

"We'd better bring the sunscreen," Tom said, pulling up a chair and plunking down his video camera.

He had decided to make a home movie of the day's trip. The prologue consisted of me and Tom sitting in deck chairs as we talked into the camera perched on the railing.

"They should be hanging around the edge of the weed line," Tom intoned for the camera.

"We'll probably find them in ten to twelve feet of water," I added.

"And they'll be real suckers for one of these six-inch, purple Hoot's worms, fished real slow," Tom concluded.

The Tom and Dave fishing show was off to a fine start. Roland Martin or Orlando Wilson never sounded so good. But as Tom was backing the trailer down into the water at the public landing, I remembered my previous perfect plans, high hopes, and professional-sounding strategies, only to have the fish refuse to cooperate. This little lake, though, certainly looked bassy. And the weed line was favorable at ten to twelve feet. I tied on a plastic worm and a one-eighth-ounce sinker, rigging it Texas style. Tom did the same.

Pitch it to the edge of the weeds, let it sink, and crawl it over the bottom. Tom must have eased the boat about two hundred yards down the shoreline with the bow-mounted trolling motor before he broke the silence. "Apparently, they're not going to jump into the boat." I allowed as how it was too early to panic.

Tom suddenly stared at his rod tip, at the tic-tic of a biting bass. Tom now wouldn't have noticed a nuclear explosion. He thrust out the rod in front of him, reeled up the slack line, and set the hook. The rod bucked, and Tom whooped. "Get some pictures of this!" I got most of it on tape, including the moment he grabbed that feisty two-pounder by the lower jaw and hoisted it into the boat.

Within the next hour he caught a dozen more fish that danced on the water and dove under the boat. I was getting damned good with the camera, trying my best to avoid looking jealous. Every time I turned that camera on and zoomed in on another fish in Tom's hand, he would say something like "Oh, son, this is a nice fish. Let me tell you how I did it."

Finally I felt that sharp tic on my rod. Pick up the slack, get a little angle on her and lean back and set that hook. My rod doubled, and I had that delicious feeling again, that bulldogging and head shaking of a bass with a set of shoulders. Tom was videotaping it all. By the time I hoisted this two-pounder aboard, I was grinning from ear to ear. I released the fish, as Tom had done with his. For the next half hour I caught all the bass. Mine also danced and dove and generally cut up.

When we took a break for lunch, a can of pop and an apple, we were giggling like schoolgirls. We were catching fish just the way we had predicted. We had the lake to ourselves, and the day was turning out not the scorcher we'd expected. All afternoon we took turns catching bass and taking pictures. I got one. Tom got one. Get the camera. By early evening I had an ache in the small of my back and a pain in my neck and shoulder. We'd been on our feet for eight hours, casting and cranking.

Tom looked back at me from the bow. "That's it," he said. "Let's call it a day." He didn't have to say it twice. We hauled the boat back onto the trailer and headed back to the cabin.

We had caught more bass than we'd cared to count, and we had released them all. We had taken our best action pictures ever.

The Journey Goes On

We had laughed all day—at each other, at ourselves and at the two of us together. We had even eaten healthily, not salami and Twinkies but pears and apples.

"You know," Tom said, "it doesn't get any better than this."

I agreed. It was a perfect day fishing. But maybe, I thought, we really had discovered the secret to bass fishing, and now we could catch them whenever we wanted.

The next morning we visited another pothole lake, deployed our secret formula, and caught one tiny bass in five hours.

Tom had been right. It really doesn't get any better than that.

The Shore-Lunch Gang

Around noon our four boats gathered and we pulled up on a tiny island in the middle of Sandpoint Lake at the edge of Voyageurs National Park.

For more than twenty years, in one form or another, we'd been gathering for shore lunches in places like this. We are a collection of former reporters, a copy editor or two and friends of friends: Mo, Lub, the Bear, Ted, Jim, Glenn, and Ron.

The island was ringed with fragrant cedars. We could see the mouth of Redhorse Bay with its rocky ledges and timber-strewn shore. Not a boat could be seen, and on this sunlit day in June I could imagine that we were the first human beings to venture this far north. Lub and Ted gathered the firewood, Jim filleted the northerns and smallmouth from our stringers, and Mo opened the cans of beans and spaghetti. As usual I was making preparations to fry the fish. We'd been doing this for so many years that everyone knew his appointed chore, and only the occasional newcomer had to be told what to do and what not to do. One time a rookie grabbed a fork to turn a fish fillet. "Nim fries the fish," Mo said with a look of stern disapproval.

We began establishing our rituals at Lower Manitou Lake in southern Ontario. At one of our earliest shore lunches there, I had to battle the Bear for a fish to fry. When we pulled up for lunch, the Bear had caught the only fish, a beautiful ten-pound northern pike that he was planning to take home. We told him his fish was shore lunch. "No, guys," he said, "this one is too pretty. I may even put it on the wall." Mo looked at me, and I looked at Lub, and the three of us pulled out our fillet knives and advanced toward the Bear. He got the idea, and after an hour or so he even quit bitching about our thievery. The fish was delicious.

Most of the time we've managed to catch enough fish. Once, in a pouring rainstorm on Eagle Lake, we couldn't get a fire started. We ate Spam on thick slices of homemade bread. Only Tommy Matthews refused to join us. "I won't do it," he said. "I won't drive four hundred miles north into the Canadian wilderness, pound five miles across a wind-swept lake, and then eat pig parts, cold, on a slice of bread. You have no pride." We asked Tommy to pass the thermos of coffee.

We do have pride in cooking shore lunch ourselves, and we can do it as well as the Ojibwa guides. The one time we allowed our camp owner to fix shore lunch was a disaster. He had the lunch planned down to the tiniest detail. We helped out by filleting the fish, opening the cans, starting the fire, and so on. By the time the fire was ready, our camp operator was furiously digging through the shore-lunch box. "I can't find the onions," he said, "to make my onion rings." The Bear smiled sheepishly and handed him a bowl of the three onions, finely diced. Our guest host gamely struggled through the lunch, but his heart wasn't in it.

Recently we've changed the menu to accommodate our increasingly delicate constitutions. We now carry as much diet pop as beer and ale. We've replaced the pound of Snowflake Lard with a bottle of peanut oil. We've even been known to bring along packets of artificial sweetener. But the fish are still fried to a golden turn. The beans come hot and bubbling from the can. The bread is thick, and the strawberry jam is sweet. The coffee is strong and hot. You balance your plate on a knee, sit on a boat cushion, and watch the lake and catch a breeze.

This year I sat on a small hill where I could look down on the group. As I watched them eat and talk, I thought, There's not a straight-line success story among the lot of us. Only half had business cards, and only one had a secretary. We hadn't flown as high or made as big a splash as we'd once hoped or dreamed, but we were better men than we used to be—better fathers, husbands, and friends. We took more time for one other. We called more often. We talked more often of things real and sometimes painful. I probably couldn't have raised ten thousand dollars in seed money from the whole assembled group, but I was far richer for their friendship.

A Sparrow among Cardinals

As the assembled faculty moved up the steps and into the chapel of the University of Saint Thomas for the president's faculty convocation, the September morning could not have been prettier, but it was maybe eighty-five degrees under clear blue skies, and I was sweating mightily under my simple black gown. I was the only one wearing basic black. The two hundred faculty members were decked out in their graduate-school colors with capes of green and gold and blue and brown and even gowns of crimson and mauve.

I was glad to be there to teach journalism. For twenty-six years I'd been a journalist: newspaper reporter, managing editor, television correspondent, and television associate news director. But I couldn't wear any of those titles around my shoulders or on my gown. My only degree was bachelor of science, which didn't entitle me to a cape or a color. I kept wondering whether my colleagues noticed me, a sparrow in a flock of cardinals.

A little speech was rattling around in my brain: "I don't have all your degrees, but I admire what you've done, and I am an intellectually curious man, and I intend to remain one at Saint Thomas." Get a grip on it, I thought. Making a speech to defend yourself against a self-inflicted put-down is the height of insecurity.

I took my seat in the chapel and listened to the invocation, the spiritual reading, and the remarks of the vice president for academic affairs. He began to present all the new full-time faculty in alphabetical order: "David C. Boyd, assistant professor of chemistry, B.A., Saint Olaf College, Ph.D., University of Minnesota; Catherine A. Craft, assistant professor of English, B.A., Canisius College, M.A., Ph.D., University of Rochester; "Kenneth E. Goodpaster, professor and holder of the Koch Chair in Business Ethics, A.B., University of Notre Dame, A.M., Ph.D., University of Michigan."

Oh, damn, I thought, he'll call my name soon, and my credentials will pass so quickly that I'll hardly have time to walk to the front of the chapel, greet the vice president, and get my copy of Saint Thomas's history.

I barely heard the names of the other new faculty. They were up to the Ms when I suddenly had a mind's-eye picture of my mother's face. She died in 1961, a year before I graduated from the University of Wisconsin. She had been proud of my performance in college. I was awarded my Phi Beta Kappa key after she died. I closed my eyes and thought, Hey, Mom, look at me. I'm sitting here with all these scholars, these doctors. What do you think of that?

I opened my eyes. I kept my head up and walked slowly when my name was called. "David H. Nimmer, instructor in journalism, B.S., University of Wisconsin."

Big Brother

Bob Shelby, big brother of the television news anchorman Don Shelby, died of complications after surgery in the late spring of 1990 in Gulfport, Mississippi. I had had the good fortune to share a bass boat with Bob and Don on several trips down south, and somehow Bob was like a big brother to me, too.

Whereas Don has the high energy and a way of bounding from place to place that can make you tired just watching, Bob just kind of eased from spot to spot. While Don looks as though he stepped out of the pages of *Gentlemen's Quarterly*, with his fitted shirts and tailored suits, Bob dressed for comfort, more like someone out of a Sears catalogue. And when Don was towing his brand-new seventeen-foot bass boat in the Aquatennial Parade, Bob was probably repairing his mongrel boat and motor with its rebuilt lower unit and secondhand prop.

But for all their differences, the Shelby brothers were as one. Don would give the punch line, and Bob would tell the joke, or vice versa. Drop a name or mention a town, and one of them would have a story that the other would finish. I especially enjoyed watching them together because I never had a brother.

One sunny Saturday on the river tidal waters near Gulfport, I was in a boat with one of Bob's bass-fishing buddies. Don and Bob were in Bob's boat, an old lime-green tri-hull, pulled on a trailer that started to shimmy at anything over fifty miles an hour. We spotted them just about noon. The fishing hadn't been very fast, and we had caught only one small bass. So we stayed a good distance away from them to avoid a razzing if their luck had been better.

Bob was on the trolling motor in the bow, and Don was standing on the casting deck in the stern. Don made a few casts, set

The Journey Goes On

the pole down, and picked up another and began casting. And then that pole Don had just set on the deck was pulled into the water. But Don said nothing to Bob, just kept on casting.

Later Don told me what had happened. He had seen a swirl on the water—perhaps a rising bass. He set down the pole with the heavier lure so he could cast a floater. The lure dangling in the water got caught on some brush, and before Don could make a move, the whole rig disappeared over the side of the boat. What to do? Tell Bob and receive a ration of verbal abuse, or ignore the loss and say nothing? Don said nothing and kept on casting. He still had three or four rods at his feet.

For several minutes Bob maneuvered the boat along the weed line. Finally he paused. "Well," he said, "do you want to go back and get that rod and reel, or do you want to leave it on the bottom of the lake?"

"Yeah," said Don, "like you can go back and find it? It's on the bottom, gone, disappeared."

Bob said he didn't need a lecture on the finer points of gravity. He just wanted to know whether his little brother wanted his rod and reel.

Bob turned the boat around and went back. He picked up his own rod and reel, rigged with a heavy jigging lure, and made a short cast. He bounced the lure up and down a couple of times and grunted. The pole bent, and he started to reel. He had snagged his brother's gear on the first cast.

He never cracked a smile as he handed the dripping equipment to Don. "Little brother, I believe this is your rod and reel."

Even after thirty years, that's what big brothers are for and that's why little brothers never forget them.

A Pocket Knife

David Olson was one of those guys you seem to have known since childhood. You knew in a moment that you could spend a day fishing with him and feel comfortable. He was short, with a round face and an easy smile. I met him at lunch one day with my old friend Tom Mihokanich. Tom and Dave worked for a downtown hospital, developing and marketing special programs.

During the course of that lunch at the Normandy Inn, I discovered that Dave had grown up in Wisconsin about thirty miles from my hometown. He too had drunk a few beers in those corner taverns that serve fish on Friday nights, and he had ridden the back roads with his buddies looking for adventure and excitement. By the time lunch was over, we'd promised to get together again to see what else we had in common, but work and commitments and life in general got in the way, and we didn't see each other for four or five months.

Eventually Tom brought us together again at the Normandy. We talked about a business trip Tom and Dave had taken to Colorado. They'd driven into the mountains, where Tom, who grew up in northeast Minneapolis, saw for the first time the grandeur of mountain passes and snow-capped peaks. Listening to the two of them, I thought that if I ever had a chance to travel with Dave Olson, I'd take it.

Within a month of our second meeting, however, doctors discovered a cancerous tumor in his brain. He began treatment immediately, and Tom told me of his progress. When Dave and I met again for lunch, this time alone, he looked well although he was thinner and grayer. He told me that he intended to "give the big C a real battle," taking whatever treatments the doctors recommended and working for as long as he had the strength. He laughed as he shook a cigarette from a pack and lit it. "For the first time in my life, I'm not worried about smoking these damn things," he said.

He and his wife were about to spend a vacation on the North Shore, and not long afterward Tom told me that Dave could no longer work and wanted to see us at his home for lunch. That's the only time I ever saw him: at lunch. On our way over to Saint Paul, Tom, who's also a health counselor, told me that Dave was realistic about his impending death and probably wanted to say goodbye. Tom knew that since my mother's death from cancer, I'd been uneasy and even frightened about death.

Dave, as he greeted us at the door, was frightening. The steroids and other medications had caused him to swell up. He looked like the Pillsbury Doughboy. I wouldn't have recognized him, except for his smile. The three of us talked for a while and ate the lunch Dave's wife had set out. Then Dave said he wanted to see each of us alone.

Dave and I sat on the couch. "I wish we could have had more time," he said. "We would have become great friends." He produced a small pocket knife and handed it to me. "This belonged to my grandfather, and I want you to have it—just something to remember me by." We both started to cry, and I hugged him and thanked him.

On our way home I told Tom that Dave had helped make dying less scary for me. We agreed that we'd never seen anyone confront death with as much candor or courage. David died within a couple of weeks after our lunch.

In the ensuing years I've thought of him once in a while. One day in the year I turned fifty, I was feeling old and awkward and hopeless. I was walking around in my backyard, and I shoved my hands into the pockets of my jeans and felt that little knife in the watch pocket. I opened the blade and rubbed it against my thumb, and I started to smile.

The Last Fishing Trip

The fall morning had dawned cloudy and cool in northern Wisconsin, and we didn't have enough time to be choosy: this was our only day to fish together. I'd dragged my boat from the Twin Cities up to Minocqua so my father and I could continue a twenty-five-year tradition. We'd been told about a little lake loaded with northern pike.

In the restaurant as we ate our bacon and eggs, I noticed that at the age of seventy-seven he was beginning to look frail. When we left the restaurant, I pulled Dad's collar up around his neck. "It's going to be cold out there," I said, "so make sure you stay warm." He reminded me that he'd avoided catching his death for almost eight decades without any help from me.

We both had stubborn streaks, and we could have been better at supporting and taking advice from each other over the years, I thought as I backed the boat trailer into the water. I put our rods and gear into the boat. This pretty little lake had a few deadfalls along the shore and a couple of patches of lily pads along the far side. "This morning," I said, "let's show them no mercy."

For the first hour we drifted along the edge of an offshore weed bed, alternately casting spoons and dragging big sucker minnows, with no luck, not even a strike. So I motored over to the lily pads and dropped the anchor. "Let's put on a couple of bobbers. We'll let these suckers swim around, and maybe some old pike will get interested."

Dad chuckled and threw his line out. I poured him a cup of coffee, and he lit a cigarette. "With the way they're biting," he said, "I think I can risk a break for a smoke."

We had the lake to ourselves. I leaned back in the boat seat and propped my feet on the gunwales. The birches were already tinged with yellow. A wedge of Canada geese flew southward. "Fall is creeping up, Dad. Maybe the northerns have moved into the real shallow water. Let's give them another fifteen minutes and then fish that creek mouth over there." I didn't hear an answer, so I turned toward Dad.

He was sitting straight as a stick. Suddenly his body started to shake. His head dropped to his chest, and his rod and reel fell into the lake. He pitched forward over the side of the boat so his face was floating in the water.

I couldn't grasp what was happening. I wanted to holler, but I couldn't make a sound. I struggled to my feet, stepped over the middle seat, and grabbed his belt. "Dad, Dad," I blurted, "what's wrong with you? What's happened to you?" I yanked his belt and rolled him into the bottom of the boat. He lay still with his mouth open and his eyes rolled back.

I thought he'd had a stroke. I tried to clear his tongue from his throat. I was struck by how cracked and brown his teeth looked. Get over it, I told myself: make sure he's breathing. He was. He looked peaceful. I put a boat cushion under his head. And then I started to cry. "Jesus, Dad. I love you. I love you. I did the best I could. I really did." He couldn't hear.

Then I realized I hadn't made a move to get help. Somehow I couldn't move any faster as I wound in my line and hauled up the anchor. Dad was still out. "God," I prayed, "if he's going to die, please let him die in this boat. Don't let him live to be a cripple."

We drifted for several minutes. Finally I started the motor and turned back to the landing. I ran to a nearby cabin and called the little hospital in Minocqua. Within twenty minutes an emergency crew was lifting Dad into an ambulance. I followed him to the hospital, where I phoned my stepmother. I drove to the motel, picked her up and sped back.

When we walked into the emergency room, Dad was on a stretcher, with an intravenous tube in his arm. He was conscious and talking. "What the hell happened?" he asked. He had no recollection of those forty-five minutes. The doctors couldn't offer much of an explanation. Maybe he had a seizure. Maybe he just blacked out. But it was not a stroke, and two days later he was back at his home in southeastern Wisconsin.

That was the last time he and I fished up north. Visiting him ten years later, I watch him sleeping in his chair, with his chin on his chest and his mouth open. His body is gnarled by arthritis. The cartilage in his hip joints is destroyed, gone. To get up from his chair, he rocks back and forth, grasps his walker, and rises slowly, whistling in pain.

So I think of that day on the lake. How much easier it would have been—I'm afraid to finish the thought. How much easier it would have been—but this way I've said to my father, to his face, "Dad, I love you."

Handful of Memories

"Damnit," Ruth muttered, "I hate cutting your father's fingernails." She was holding a small pair of scissors in one hand and his index finger in the other. My stepmother has a mild case of palsy, and Dad has a severe case of arthritis. It's not a good combination for cutting nails.

Yet as I watched Ruthie's awkward and sometimes painful attempts, I hesitated to take over. I didn't want to cut my father's fingernails: that would just reinforce his helplessness. But finally I heard myself say, "Let me do that." Carefully, gingerly, I picked up Dad's right hand. The fingers were bent and the knuckles swollen. His veins stood out like interstate highways on a road map. His hand was cold but soft, even delicate. I was nervous. "Relax Dad," I mumbled. "I've never lost anyone so far."

I started with his thumb. Slowly I clipped the edges of the nail. Neither of us said a word. My mind was suddenly filled with memories of my father and where those hands had been. I remembered the vegetable garden behind our garage where Dad worked on his knees with a trowel in his hand. He knelt on a board and used a string to make a straight row for his radishes, carrots, beans, onions, and lettuce. He placed each radish seed about an inch apart in a trench row. He was always absorbed and relaxed, as relaxed as he ever got. He planted a good garden, and he knew it. It gave him pleasure, and he showed it. Every half hour or so, he'd take a break from his planting, shake a cigarette from the pack, and light up. He'd take a drag, hold the cigarette in front of his mouth, and survey his handiwork. The old boy had the hands of a gardener.

He also had the instincts of a hunter, and sometimes on Sunday mornings in October I walked the hardwoods with him. His right hand would be wrapped around the stock of his twelve-gauge shotgun, while his left hand, under the muzzle, was ready to pump a shell into the chamber. I didn't like to hunt much, but I liked to walk, so I was Dad's squirrel dog, except that Dad could spot them in the branches before I had any inkling they were there. "To your left, Dave," Dad would whisper, "on the very top branch. See him?" I'd look up and follow Dad's pointing finger, but it usually took a few moments before I'd spot the squirrel. Then Dad would have me walk around the tree, to spook the squirrel over to his side and into shotgun range. Dad would snap the gun up to his shoulder, aim, and fire. More often than not, a fat fox squirrel or gray squirrel hit the ground. Dad said that his cousin Franklin was a much better shot, but I was always proud of his prowess.

Especially when athletics were involved—like the time when he was almost sixty-five and pitched seven innings of softball. It was at the company picnic, and Dad was on top of his game. He'd stare down at the batter, hold the ball in front of his belt, swing his right hand behind his back, and loft the ball toward the plate. His teammates said it was "good to have Nimmy on the mound because he doesn't fart around—he throws strikes."

At work those hands moved faster. As the circulation manager at the newspaper, Dad was in charge of the carrier boys. One of his jobs was counting out papers, almost ten thousand of them, to one hundred carriers. They'd stand in a line in front of a long table.

"Schultz," Dad would holler, "how many papers do you need?"

"Ninety-two."

Dad would grab a huge stack of newspapers, bounce them up and down a couple of times to even them off, and start counting. "Two, five, eight, twelve." His fingers would fly over the top of the stack, and Lord help the carrier who did anything to interrupt his count. When he got to ninety-two, he'd heave that pile of newspapers toward the carrier. I always wondered how he had the strength to toss around twenty-five or thirty pounds of newspapers, but I never wondered how he could count so fast: it was those nimble fingers dancing across ten thousand newspapers a day.

Occasionally those fingers did some disciplining. Dad would put his hand around my shoulder and turn me to face the result of my misdeeds. "Right over there," he'd say, pointing with the index finger of his right hand. "See the corner of the garage window? Looks like a crack to me." He knew we'd been playing touch football in the backyard the night before. I always figured it would be pretty hard to put one over on the old man, but that never stopped me from trying. Although Dad pointed and gestured, he never struck or spanked me. He didn't have to: one wag of that finger was enough to make his point.

Those hands, however, didn't always have that authoritative touch when they were wrapped around a rod and reel. Dad loved to fish, but he never fished enough to get over the jitters when a big one struck. One early fall morning we were fishing a bass lake in Michigan's Upper Peninsula with Dad's guide and friend Ted Eberly in his canoe. Dad was casting a surface plug, as far as his old closed-face Zebco reel would allow. Suddenly he got a strike, and his rod almost doubled over as he furiously wound the reel handle. The rod and reel were just under his chin, but Dad couldn't stop winding long enough to take a breath or lower the works to his lap for more comfort and control. No, Dad was a human winch, a gray-haired derrick, bound and determined to bring that smallmouth bass to the net. And she was a big one—maybe four pounds, Ted said, as she broke water about ten feet from the canoe. Dad cranked harder and brought her too close: he didn't leave enough line between the bass and the rod tip. One final lunge at the canoe and she snapped the line, making off with his three-dollar balsa floater. His hands were shaking as he lit a cigarette.

And now his left hand in mine was shaking as I tried to finish trimming his fingernails. "Ouch," he hollered. "You cut that too close."

"Just hold still," I ordered. "I'm about finished, and I've got to tell you, Dad, this is a professional-looking manicure I've given you."

I held his hands up for him to see, and I looked them over, and I looked at my own. They were beginning to look like his.